SILENT ANGEL

Antonia Arslan

SILENT ANGEL

Translated by Siobhan Nash-Marshall

IGNATIUS PRESS
San Francisco

AUGUSTINE INSTITUTE
Greenwood Village, CO

Cover Design: Lisa Patterson

ISBN 978-1-950939-13-8 (pbk)
ISBN 978-1-64229-123-0 (eBook)
Library of Congress Control Number 2020935316
Printed in Canada ∞

"We passed in front of the lowered shutters, the closed tea houses, the abandoned homes of Armenians, and the luminously icy shop windows; below the chestnut tree and poplars covered in snow; and walking through we heard the noise of our footsteps through the sad streets lit by a few neon lights ..."

Orhan Pamuk, *Snow*

Acknowledgments

From the bottom of my heart, I would like to thank the following people for their suggestions, friendship, and precious help: Kohar Sahakian, granddaughter of a survivor from the valley; Rita Mahdessian, who read me the essential *History of the Land of Taron* by Karo Sasuni (Beirut: Sevan, 1956), in Armenian; Marina Pasqui, Teresa Tentori, and Isabella Vettorel; Siobhan Nash-Marshall and Sona Haroutyunian, as always; and lastly Ela Tokay for her smile and Eileen Romano for everything.

Chapter One

The monastery was in flames. For miles, the red spot danced frantically, seeming to wane for a bit, only to flare up. For miles, the people around it stared, gripped by shapeless, slithering fear, or by frenetic animation. The prominent position high up on the mountain of the sacred site of *Sourp Arakelots Vank*, Holy Apostles' Monastery, made the blaze visible from the entire valley. You could almost hear the cries of the hunted monks and catch the terrible smells of their scorched long beards, of their tunics that were set on fire with the men still inside of them.

Makarios the Greek crossed the village in a hurry and, taking streets known only to him, reached the house of the midwife, his old friend Eleni. They were both from the Chora of Paros. They had been children together, and their mothers had wanted them to marry. But Makarios, the rambunctious son of the cobbler, had run away when he was still very young. Eleni, who was filled with shame, ended up in Ionia, and the

1

nuptial garlands were never woven. After years of wandering, they finally both ended up in the fertile plains of Moush in Anatolia and settled amongst the Armenians. They were happy to get together every once in a while, and they treated each other with utmost respect. Good people, the obstinate and kind *Moushetsi*, "but blind kittens, like all Armenians," Eleni repeats on her rounds through the families, as she tries to shake them out of their torpid passivity. "Everything passes, even the Red Sultan; this war too will pass," the village women tell her in a whisper. Many of them have husbands, fiancées, or relatives in America, working hard so that they can buy homes and hoping not to make their promised ones wait too long for them. Many women also have children on the front line. And yet, war or no war, it is already summer. There are festivals for the harvest and for the first grapes, and all of the women have plans and thoughts of celebration.

Enclosed within its circle of mountains, like in an enchanted ring, lies the very fertile valley of Daron, where, as the proverb claims, "the land and water are sweet." Rich in churches and villages, and whose main city is Moush (*mshush* is "fog" in Armenian), it maintains its traditions and thousand-year-old rites. It is a secluded highland that has been one of the centers of Armenian civilization since its first centuries. Saint Gregory, called "the Illuminator," who in 301 converted King Tiridates with all of his people to Christianity, founded the Holy Apostles Monastery here, and it houses the sacred relics of the first Apostles that were brought from Rome and have been venerated throughout the centuries.

The Armenian people have learned to bow their heads when persecution rears its head, to shut themselves up in opaque silence, to disconnect from their own thoughts, and then slowly to get back up. Like stalks of wheat, after a storm has crushed but not broken them, they sway in the breeze the next day. But the monastery fire has something so permanent and threatening about it that Makarios feels the need for advice.

"They're coming, my Eleni," he shouts breathlessly as he reaches the front door. "The Third Army is coming. They are retreating after their defeats in the Caucasus. This time it's much worse: Turkish soldiers are furious and have become nasty." Makarios gets by, and rather well, as a jack-of-all-trades for whoever hires him. He is always ready to deliver a message, fix a window, keep an eye on an empty house, and he is such an easy and smooth talker that he conquers the reserved, proud inhabitants of the valley. These inhabitants, the Armenians of the mountains, who know every nuance of the art of farming, are so full of that age-old diffidence toward any kind of civil authority that they often fall prey to surly embarrassment, or desperate silence.

Makarios is always the first in the know and is usually everyone's newsman. But not this time. With his cunning mediator's instinct he has understood that there is something dark and sinister in the air, and he goes straight to Eleni, his friend and wise confidante, who always calms him down by talking about the Panagia of Paros and the crystal-like cove of their childhood, where the purest spring water bubbled up alongside the seashore.

In the quiet hours of the afternoon, if she is around, she sits on the veranda under a grapevine, with her hands on her lap and her eyes half-closed. But tonight she is nowhere to be seen. Makarios enters the house, anxiously crosses the kitchen and the inner room, and finds her curled up on the floor in a corner of the balcony in the back, staring at something. Then he sees it, the red spot of fire dancing in the distance, and understands that Eleni already knows that the distant flames mark the end.

"The monastery is on fire; it's been on fire for hours," he tells her in a low voice. "What will happen now? What will the Armenians do? It's an ominous sign, you know? It is one of their most sacred sites; it was founded by the great Saint Gregory. And it was ransacked twenty years ago. What do they think they'll find there now?"

"I wasn't here yet," Eleni whispers, sighing, "but that time all of the monks were killed, and now only the abbot and two monks are left."

Neither one says what he is really thinking. It is the end of that serene life, of evenings enjoying a sip of *oghi* and a bowl of nuts. The apocalypse of that far-off war covering Europe with blood is approaching: the Russians are advancing, and the Turks retreating, determined to make a clean sweep of things. Then there are the rumors about the Armenians, which are not easy to ignore, especially when the merchants at the bazaar have begun to refuse to sell them things on credit.

And there are all of the new faces of the Turks who had withdrawn from Macedonia and Bulgaria wandering through the streets, Makarios thinks. They are famished, and God only knows where they hole up. His thought collides with Eleni's, who has seen where they live, in the dark and dirty tobacco warehouses, where they pass their days sharpening their knives and spewing curses at Westerners and their lackeys.

The circle of mountains that surrounds them suddenly no longer feels like that natural wondrous wall built by the divinity to protect the fertile plain, with its slow rivers, fluctuating fogs, gigantic trees, and, beyond the peaks, Ararat always blanketed in snow—an invisible guardian. Now it feels like the lip of a giant net that traps all of the inhabitants of the valley.

A new distrust burrows its way into their souls as they sit side by side, contemplating the faraway fire. Their hands seek each other. Makarios clears his throat and says, "Bring me a shot of *oghi*, Eleni. Let's toast to life. And then let's eat something and start packing our bags, in silence."

"Are you crazy?" Eleni protests. "You want us to leave? No one has threatened us yet."

"Exactly," replies Makarios. "Why wait for the knife, like lambs to be sacrificed? We need to escape before we are swept up in the fate of the Armenians. They will be shown no mercy here."

Now Eleni sees the clouds becoming dyed in red; she hears distant screams—the harbingers of doom—and shudders. She looks at her little house, its front lawn, the majestic plane tree and the little spring, the flowering garden with its lettuce, purple eggplant, and zucchini that have grown disproportionately this year, and the rows of gerania neatly arranged at the windows as well as the colorful zinnias—the pride of her rustic gardening.

"As you wish, Makarios," she sighs. "In the end, you always manage to get me to do what you want." She smiles, appeased. If it is true that even in the most tragic moments affection is consoling, then at that moment, despite everything, Eleni is happy.

Chapter Two

They climb down to the river, crossing through the woods, to take a swim. It has been an extremely hot day, and under the scarves that they had knotted low on their necks Anoush and Kohar sweat profusely. Anoush, delicate and slender, is already the mother of three children, all of whom are fortunately healthy. The youngest has already been weaned. Kohar has dark hair and broad shoulders and is powerful and curvaceous. Her fiancé is a carpenter, who silently adores her and patiently puts up with her scolding. They are thinking of getting married in the fall at the monastery's great festival.

Both women have corsets around their waists and wear coarse cotton blouses. Once they reach the river, they quickly undress, pile their clothes under a big flat rock, and—as they have many other times—plunge into the ice-cold water of the Aratsani River, squealing with delight. The local women know that there is always a veil of fog on the river, and they take advantage of it, swimming naked. That corner, where the boiling water subsides and makes a tortuous bend and is filled with reeds and wild anemones, is their favorite spot. Further up, the water stagnates in swamps that have been cleaned up and are used to irrigate the fields. The entire plain of Moush is lush, set as it is between two rivers that surround it in a somewhat languid and almost sensual embrace, flowing slowly before abandoning it.

In the evening after work, or sometimes at noon, when the heat rages, they all go to the river, even the older women.

But today Anoush and Kohar are alone and do not ask themselves why. They had worked hard in the cellar of the big farm far from the village, cleaning vats and preparing the jars that will be used to store vegetables for the winter. The famous *khmi*, the prickly asparagus, and the gigantic beans were almost ripe; soon, old Serpuhi will tell them when the phase of the moon is right, and then the canning will begin.

They have not raised their heads, nor have they looked at the mountains. As soon as they had finished lining up the containers upside down, they had washed their hands and had run to the river. They want to be alone; they have important things to talk about. Anoush's husband wants to go to America, to the far west—California. They already have friends there, and they can make money. Kohar advises her not to let him go alone. What if he meets another woman, a skillful one, who makes his head spin like one of those shady ladies who play dice and took part in the gold rush in the wild Klondike?

Kohar had read an article about the Klondike in a French magazine and is convinced that a good girl from Moush cannot compete with the glamour of Klondike, which she envisions as a huge city full of lights and nightclubs. But Anoush argues passionately: "If I have to go, then the children have to come with me. And you too, with your carpenter. We'll become a family and help each other." She has always leaned on Kohar and her strength. They were schoolmates and still sing together in the church choir.

Fantasizing and splashing in the water, hours pass. A rosy mist envelops them. "I need to go," Anoush says. "It's late. I need to run to the children; my mother-in-law will complain."

"Yes," Kohar sighs, "you're right. It's starting to cool off. But let me stay five more minutes, and I'll try to find a couple of crabs under the big stone." She quickly dives down without waiting for an answer. She knows that Anoush will never leave by herself.

Just so, her friend follows her, laughing and waving her arms clumsily. Her loose hair flows down like fresh curtains on either side of her face. A lark sings in the distance; the cicada grow crazy under the sun.

The two women will always remember that moment, when time had stopped for them, and the water, the earth, and the light of the lost land gave them one last embrace.

Chapter Three

At that very moment both women hear a rhythmic sound approaching fast from up the river. It is galloping horses. Realizing that they have no time to get dressed, they instinctively withdraw toward the small flat island in the middle of the current and hide among the reeds. They gather their hair in one hand, breathe quietly, and cower. With the other hand, they cling onto a clump of grass, and, like those children who think they cannot be seen if they keep their eyes closed, do not look at the riverbank.

Each bitterly reproaches herself for having taken this mortal risk. Who are the approaching horsemen? Surely they are not Armenians. The Armenians do not have horses, nor would they ride so brashly, approaching like a loud thunderstorm. *They might be Kurds*, they think. After all, the Kurds do have horses, and every once in a while they descend into the valley from their eagle's nests in the mountains, causing a stir, scaring the farmers, making off with a calf—or even, at times, amusing themselves with a girl who is to be married.

But, behind the gallop, they hear a dull and confused rumble, the trampling of a thousand feet, echoed by a thud, almost as if a whimper escaped from the trodden earth. Everything seems to be hushed with fear. Even the mist, which had protected them till now, lifts.

With the birds and the cicadas silenced, even the river seems to hold its breath. Anoush and Kohar feel cold and frightened. The horsemen come closer; the noise becomes unbearable; their hearts thump. A stiff hand, Anoush's, loses its grip; then a foot slips on the moss. Anoush would have let the river carry her off, but Kohar grabs her wrist, shakes it, and signals for them to slide silently into the water.

With their minds in flame and hearts desperate, they watch trembling as the remnant of the Ottoman Third Army that survived the harsh battles against the Russian army in the Caucuses marches alongside the river. Behind the still pride-filled cavalry, the troops show signs of fatigue and uneasiness, nursing the scars of wounds inflicted by men in hostile and unknown lands, and the despondency of confidence lost.

They are going to quarter in the fertile plains of Moush to lick their wounds and to avenge their wounded and abused pride, harboring a deaf rage that seeks a target. And there they will find the ready scapegoat, the Armenians, the internal enemy.

Anoush and Kohar know nothing about this. They only feel fear, ancestral fear, the insuppressible fear of the lamb before the wolf.

Evening finally descends, and a red, bloody, mysterious, beautiful moon rises. Under the cover of the relative gloom, the two women with great effort drag themselves out of the water and wait, holding each other, shivering, and counting every minute. But the soldiers never stop coming; and after the troops, it is the turn of the wagons transporting the wounded, the munitions, and the victuals. So when every noise is spent, the moon has already set. It is completely dark.

Moving silently in the shadows, they find their clothes under the stone, quickly dress, and set off for the village as cautiously as possible through the woods. The road is long, but the two girls do not speak. They are gripped by growing anxiety. "It's too quiet, Kohar," Anoush whispers, shuddering. "Why can't we hear anything?"

"They must be going around, helping the soldiers," Kohar hurriedly replies. "You'll see. They're going again to take our livestock, and all of our things! We need to go to America, get away from here, and quickly!"

Chapter Four

As they near the end of the woods, they begin to see a hazy red light winking at them through the trees. It grows with every step. It is the shy and sensible Anoush who first understands: "Mother of God, it's a fire! That's why there's no one around. They must all be there helping out." Such is the village's typical response to a house on fire. The houses are made of wood and stone, and the risk of fire is always present. But the flames are up high on the mountain. "It's not a house. It's the monastery!" Kohar exclaims. "The monastery is on fire! The soldiers have gone all the way there. They are burning the Holy Apostles. God have mercy on us."

"Let's hurry," Anoush suggests. "Four more arms are always useful." Both girls begin to run fretfully toward the nearest houses. They have always lived near each other. Only a steep ramp, a right-angled turn, and four steps are left to reach the courtyard the two families share.

It is dark and empty there. Not even old Serpuhi and the brazier she always holds in her lap is there.

She is eighty years old and has certainly not gone up the mountain to put out the fire. They hear nothing. The courtyard seems uninhabited in that dense obscurity. The two women move close to each other and try, in vain, to see something. All of a sudden they hear what sounds like an almost supernatural moan, like that of a lost soul wandering on the border between worlds. Leaning on each other, Anoush and Kohar slowly make their way toward the sound and nearly stumble over a bundle. "Stop!" Anoush yells. "There's something here."

They bend down and run their fingers over it and realize that it is a cloth, and wrapped in the cloth is a child. But who is he? Anoush's youngest child does not yet know how to speak, and there are other children that age in the courtyard. Kohar's sister has a little girl who is only a month older than her boy. "But she already speaks!" yells Anoush with a stammer. "This is my son; it's Krikor. I can feel it." She quickly gathers the bundle and presses it to her heart. But the cries of before have ceased, and caressing that little head, Anoush feels something soft and wet between her fingers.

Kohar also caresses that little body, prizing him gently from Anoush's arms. She puts him on the ground, and makes the Sign of the Cross over him. She then sits on the ground, pulls Anoush toward her, holds her tight. "Now cry, but cry silently," she whispers. "This son of yours is dead. We need to focus on surviving and searching for the others."

Anoush suffocates a sob with a gurgling moan and throws herself flat on the body of her son, whispering sweet words: "I will never again wash your beautiful little feet, my little lamb, apple of my eye. I have no more milk to give you. How can I warm you now? Mother can no longer rock you."

She then covers his head with a flap of the blanket, straightens up, and looks around in the darkness. Armenian mothers have always had to deal dry-eyed with the deaths of their children; centuries of oppression and servitude have taught them. Now both Anoush and Kohar know that something terrible has happened, that it has something to do with the soldiers who marched along the river. And Anoush knows well that she cannot keep on crying for her dead son and that there is nothing left to do but to entrust him to the powers of Heaven. She now has to think about the other two. Where are they? She and her husband, Yeghishé, named their daughter Élise for good luck, as her name means "Pledged to God" in French. Hrant, the firstborn son, her little eaglet, is six years old. He is as strong and proud as a bull, and he follows his father everywhere.

The night is so dark that one can hardly see the stars and their twinkling. The two women sit next to each other in the gloom. Kohar has been quiet for a while, mindful of her friend's pain. "Let's hold each other's hands and get out on the road," she suggests. "There is no one left here, and if old Serpuhi is still in some corner of the courtyard, she's surely dead and needs nothing."

Thus with the bundle of little Krikor, they go forth feeling their way along the perimeter wall, following imperceptible traces until they reach the other entrance on the road to the high quarter on the hill. They know that right before the large entrance, in the middle of the massive wall, there is a large niche where the guard would sleep in ancient times, when the large gates were closed.

They leave Krikor there, swaddled in his bloody blanket, after a hasty prayer. Other children of the fertile plains of Moush shared his fate: strewn with kerosene and torched with their mothers in the barns, or buried alive with their mouths filled with dirt. But I would like, in my own way, to sing of the memory of at least this little one. There rises from my heart, with new words, the heart-wrenching echo of that most tender, powerful elegy of innocence and youth that I learned many years ago: "Buried along with the first dead, lies the son of Armenia / coiled around his long friends, / the ageless grain, the dark veins of his mother, / hidden inside the oblivious water / of the murmuring Arostani. / After the first death, there is no other."[1]

---

1   Citation by heart of the last stanza of a famous poem by Dylan Thomas, "A Refusal to Mourn the Death, by Fire, of a Child in London."

Chapter Five

Kohar stops. It makes no sense to leave at night as they are. They need to be strong and go home to look for a lantern, some warm clothes, and a bit of food. She forces Anoush, who is consumed by blind anguish and wants to run away, to follow her and to calm down. Kohar's house is close. It is easier to find. Feeling their way along the perimeter wall, step-by-step, they arrive at the front door. It is open. Their eyes have grown somewhat used to the dark; they can distinguish darker and lighter shadows. They catch familiar shapes. Kohar touches the doorjambs with careful fingers. She recognizes them and enters, holding Anoush by the hand.

Inside too, there is darkness and silence. But there is something else, a primitive feel of desertion and danger. After a few steps, keeping close to the walls, there is a rustle: something soft touches Kohar's leg. She stifles a cry, and looks down to see the housecat. But when Kohar, who recognizes it, bends down to pet it, the little animal freezes, arches its back, and hisses. Kohar understands. There is a foreign, hostile presence in her house, and the cat, like a protective numen, wants to warn her.

In that abrupt silence, she hears breathing in the other room. It is not her father, nor is it her mother, little brothers, grandfather, or grandmother. Kohar would recognize them, the familiar smells and noises, the sundry snoring, the inviting warmth of bodies lying on mats around the fireplace. Her shaken mind picks up on the danger signal that the cat had transmitted, and she registers darkness, emptiness, desolation, and someone, a stranger, breathing—and turning—uneasy in his deep sleep.

"There is a soldier here; where did everyone go?" she whispers to herself. Moving cautiously, she hurries to grab the big blanket that is usually rolled up in front of the *tonir*, and her father's leather jacket that hangs on a nail right above the circular fireplace with his boots lined up below it. She takes everything, even the lantern hanging on the nearby nail. Then she searches in the corner behind the fireplace, where her mother always keeps a pair of aprons and a house dress.

A bit consoled by the feel of familiar things, she squeezes the hand of Anoush, who has not moved and is clutching her skirt. She tiptoes out and climbs quietly down to the cellar, where there is, fortunately, no one.

There, calmly but quickly, like a person possessed by a silent fury, she lights the lantern, finds a bag, and fills it with bread. Luckily, the week's bread was made yesterday. She grabs a wheel of cheese and a *gavourma*,[1] her grandfather's little knife (which is always on the wooden cutting board ready to slice things), the big flask, a jar of pomegranate peel, and a handful of apricots from the shelf of drying fruit.

She ties multiple aprons around her waist, and she fills their many pockets with a bit of everything. She well knows—in the bottom of her heart—that she is saying goodbye to her home and perhaps even her land. And so, at the last minute, she places the carved wooden angel that hangs over the cellar door in her inside pocket, close to her heart—the very pocket where her mother always kept sweets for the children. It was an old gift from Melkon the mule driver, who was caught by surprise by the snow in the area years ago. He had lost his faithful mule, asked her grandfather for help, and was hosted by the family for the whole winter.

Kohar sighs, thinking about the snow and happy winter evenings as she glances over at the small sleigh with the hundred little bells hanging on the wall in the back. Her father had built it for her tenth birthday. She still stubbornly hopes that her family had the time to escape toward the mountains of Sassoun. Then she energetically ties another apron around Anoush's waist and fills up her pockets too.

---

1   Sausage made of beef and lamb, cooked for a long time, and boiled down in gelatin.

Anoush, still in shock, lets her do it. She moves only after Kohar loads the bag on her shoulders and slowly climbs the stairs of the cool cellar. She grabs a pickaxe from the wall and places it across her shoulders after having quietly tested its sharpness.

Chapter Six

And thus they leave in the night, cautiously, walking close to the walls. The entire village seems deserted. *Where to go?* Kohar asks herself feverishly. It is she who must decide. Anoush will only follow her, mutely. She stops if Kohar stops, and she takes up walking only after Kohar does, but not right away. It takes her time. It is as though she has to force herself to come back to her senses. She sighs, breathes heavily, but does not say a word.

They take the straight road that heads toward the fountain and the market square. Far off, on the hill, the fire burns vigorously. In the great and ancient Monastery of the Holy Apostles—one of the most important centers of Armenian culture—there is much to burn, besides the monks. There are vestments, icons, illuminated manuscripts of the great school of the Daron region, inlayed chests, the magnificent altar cloths of the Mother Church, and heavy damasks donated by a pious queen.

The flames seem to wane for a moment, only to pick back up vigorously amid sparks and sudden flashes of light. It is an apocalyptic vision, but for some reason that light, that heat, attracts them. *There have to be some people over there*, they think. Perhaps they have all gone up the hill to put out the fire, as they did twenty years ago when the monastery was sacked and many monks were killed.

In the threatening silence that surrounds them, the two women continue to walk, climbing up the hill. They pass by houses, all of which seem empty: eyes of denser darkness within the night. They feel increasingly anxious.

Once they reach the big square, they do not dare cross it. It is best to climb up, close to the walls, so no one notices them. "But where are all of those soldiers?" Kohar asks herself. "Have they already moved on to another village?" Having raised her voice for a moment, she pauses, intimidated by the heavy silence that surrounds them. "You can only hear the voices of the dead around here," she mutters.

But from the workshop of Sarkis the blacksmith, on the corner of the square, there shines a feeble light. Kohar heads toward it cautiously. The door is unhinged, and scattered on the ground lie the pieces of vases once filled with brilliantly colored geraniums that the blacksmith's wife, the timid Verjin, knows how to grow with keen wisdom. She loves to arrange them in floral landscapes, and she changes the arrangements daily to match her mood. She speaks little and communicates through her flowers. Everyone in the village goes to her for advice and cuttings.

The two women hear no one. There is only that light. Avoiding the pieces of terra-cotta, soil, and trampled flowers, Kohar signals to Anoush to stop, and she proceeds toward the threshold. Silence becomes a sinister, ominous pall, but Anoush obediently waits for interminable moments until Kohar reappears sobbing with eyes wide open: "They're all dead in there. Don't go in. There is blood all over the walls. They killed Sarkis with his mallet. Verjin is naked, covered with Sarkis's blood. He tried to protect her. They purposely placed the lamp next to her, so that anyone who enters sees her body."

"But where are the children?" Anoush asks alarmed. "They have two children, Julia and Hovsep."

"I saw Julia," Kohar said through tears, reluctantly adding, "She was killed by her mother."

"And Hovsep?" Anoush insists. "He always plays with my children. Let's go and see. Maybe he's hiding somewhere." She sets forth resolutely.

Reluctantly, Kohar follows her. They find him, little Hovsep, hidden in the cellar under an upended wheelbarrow. His eyes are open, and he is not hurt; but he seems to see nothing and does not react, except with a mournful squeak, when the two women pick him up in their arms and try to speak to him. He hangs like a deadweight. "We can't take him with us," Kohar says. "We can't carry him."

She tries to put him back down, but the boy grabs onto her with incredible strength. His fingers are like hooks that pierce her skirt. Anoush watches her intently. Kohar pulls him off, pries his hands from her dress, and crisply barks: "Keep quiet and walk. Come with us, but don't fall behind. We will not turn around for you. And make sure you don't cry." Hovsep looks at her, is impressed, and obeys. He nods, rubs his eyes, and starts to walk behind the women without looking back.

Chapter Seven

Now Kohar finally understands what that soft, sweet, cloying smell is that has accompanied them since they entered the village. It is blood, fresh blood that was recently shed. It becomes more and more intense, and is flowing from the village toward the outlying fields. How long will it take for beasts to come, attracted by that rich aroma? How long will it take the flies and worms to begin the banquet?

There is no returning; this Kohar well understands. The houses that had been brutally raped, desecrated by violence and death, have begun to close in on themselves, to guard the secrets of their dead. They have become tombs, miserable tombs. They will no longer give warmth and shelter to the living. The lowly objects and simple things that constituted that whole which was the life of the village with its customs— jars for fragrant herbs; pitchers of water for the wayfarer; rolled-up mats for shared sleep; underground ovens, the *tonirs*; the ancient church with its lace-like reliefs;

the poor school; the stone crosses; the thousand-year-old *khatchkars* placed outside the village by ancestors to ward off evil; the watering trough where peaceful, crescent-horned oxen would linger at night, while they watched the moon reflected in the water—everything, *everything*, would be destroyed and pillaged.

Much later, years and years later, when the echoes of the bones of the dead and their curses were spent, the most beautiful stones, fragments of sculptures, and carved symbols would be used for other buildings, other homes; and the angel with the trumpet from the pediment of the Church of the Savior would become the cornerstone of the most important building of the Kurdish encampment nearby. Of the thousands of Armenian villages in the plains of Moush, only the names would endure in the memories of the few survivors in exile, in the lyrics of nostalgic songs.

It is only very high up in the Taurus Mountains near Sassoun that the remains of a few abandoned villages still exist today. Up there, only the wind, stones, and grass are to be found. No roofs, doors, windows, or vestiges of chimneys—only empty orbits, the black holes of the ancient perforations, through which ghosts gaze and under which a coiled snake rests in the sun.

But at that moment, Kohar does not think about the future. She only knows that she has to go on toward the hill, dragging along a woman and a boy, who can be of no help to her. They must not stop at any cost. Who knows how many other soldiers are sleeping in the abandoned homes, unmindful of the blood, just enjoying the beds of the dead? And dawn will not wait too much longer to break. Woe unto them, if they are in sight when it does. So the little group walks, step after step, toward the fire on the mountain. The bag is heavy. "What did I put in it, rocks?" Kohar mumbles. "Mother of Christ, help me. I am thirsty and have worn-out arms, but I can't stop, not now. And I have to find shelter before it is too late." In her troubled mind, she makes feverish plans, none of which includes her brothers, her mother, or Anoush's children or husband. She has already folded her fiancé into the bottom of her heart. "They are lost, lost. Everyone is lost." She is sure of it, but she does not let herself cry.

They finally reach the last homes. The smell of blood remains and intensifies, like a path drawn by the murderers, who had worked their way from the most remote part of the village to the valley, near the river, and up the hill. Once up the hill, the thick poplar trees that tower over the last homes and the small circular fishpond called "The Lake of the Beautiful Miller" open up in front of them, as if inviting them into an embrace. There is a timid hint of light in the air. The birds are still silent, and yet they seem to be on the verge of calling out to each other.

Even the fire up toward the monastery seems to be dying. Kohar decides to go around the fishpond toward the huge stone mass that looms over it on the far end. Behind it, in the cool air, on the ever-moist grass, a small spring gushes up and fills an ancient marble basin. In front of it stand a stone bench and a wash basin so old that the well-carved tufa blocks surrounding it are worn down and covered with crosses that were carved into them by wayfarers and pilgrims who commemorated their last stop before the great sanctuary of the Holy Apostles. There, they would all plunge into the exceptionally cool water to bathe and make themselves worthy of the holy relics that awaited them in the sacred site blessed by the memory of the Saint Illuminator who founded it.

Kohar sits down and lets the bag fall to the ground. She bends down to drink, and she drinks and drinks. She cannot wash away the metallic taste of blood. Next comes Anoush, who drinks in silence, and, finally, little Hovsep. Anoush takes his head in her hands and puts his little face in the water that gleams in the twilight. As in a ritual cleansing, the drops skim over his eyes and cheeks and wash away his memories and anguish: a simple blessing.

They fall asleep all together, their heads on the bag and their aprons pulled over their heads; and in that cool green niche, the huge poplar trees bend down whispering in their sleep. An angel descends upon the stone mass and opens his great green wings, covering them with a protective shadow.

Chapter Eight

They are not alone. On the other side of the great erratic mass that has overlooked the calm fountain for thousands of years, the two Greeks, Makarios and Eleni, are camped out for the night. They barely managed to escape the destiny of the village inhabitants in time. They had been quicker than the soldiers, who would certainly not have distinguished between Armenians and Greeks, especially because there have never been many Greeks in those parts. The plain of Moush is too far east for the Greeks. There are, at most, only a few of them—mostly smugglers or spies. The Greeks live on the coasts: in the florid villages of the Pontus, the Black Sea, or on the Aegean coast, whose fertile lands and possibility of income had attracted many of them from Crete and the arid islands after the independence of Greece.

It had been so simple: Makarios had gotten wind of the danger, and Eleni had followed her heart. They took refuge in that well-protected corner near the fishpond, behind the fountain, a place where both had often stopped and picnicked. From up there, they had heard the troops arrive. They heard the cries, the pleas, the moans, and then the silence. They had huddled together, trembling, but in the end had fallen asleep. There was nothing else to do. One cannot wander about in a night so filled with horror. One must not disturb the frightened souls of those who have just died, and died violently. They sleep deeply and in peace, together for the very first time, holding each other's hands.

The sun has been up for a while when Kohar stirs. She lifts her head, rubs her eyes, and looks about lazily, before remembering and shuddering. She plunges her head in the water to dispel those horrible nightmares. She knows that the road toward salvation is narrow and dangerous. They have been lucky until now. But the sun is already high, and all it would take for them to be discovered is a soldier taking cover in the woods to relieve himself.

Calmly and gently she strokes Anoush's cheek. Her friend opens her eyes, remembers, and starts to cry. Kohar sees that she had held little Hovsep's hand in her sleep and is still holding it. She wakes him too, covering his mouth with her hand so he doesn't make a sound. The child is careful not to. He seems to be completely awake. His eyes dart left and right, like a little wild animal's. Then he splashes some water on his face and, by signaling, asks her for some bread.

Right then a ruffled head pops out from behind the other side of the boulder. It is Eleni, who runs her fingers through her hair and yawns with pleasure. For an infinite moment, they stare at each other probingly—the child, the young woman, and the midwife—and no one speaks. Then behind Eleni a man appears, Makarios, and Kohar recognizes them, both of them, and sighs in relief. Deeply and cathartically. Finally, a real, concrete presence that fends off the nightmares of the empty houses, the blood, and the dead.

The two Greeks also breathe more easily. Quickly, without saying a word, they all freshen their faces and hands in the cold water of the fountain, pick up their bags, and quietly walk into the thick of the poplar trees. The goal, for all of them, is the monastery. "But before getting there," Kohar whispers, "let us stop for a moment and think about what we should do. Even if we join forces, there are only five of us against that huge curse—five ill-assembled creatures." And they do not know where to go, how to escape. The high plateau of Moush is an immense valley that is fertile and rich with water, but it is surrounded on all sides by inhospitable peaks and crests. What direction should they take? Toward the mountains of Sassoun (our people know how to defend themselves in that eagle's nest) or toward Ararat and Russia?

Traveling by night, they would avoid dangerous encounters, but one's hearing sharpens in the dark, and the detachments of troops have placed sentries around them, sentries who are trained to pick up on any suspicious rustle. But moving by day would make them visible from afar in the plains that are swept by winds and bereft of trees, and they could only hope for a cloaking fog by the rivers, where people were most likely to be.

The inhabitants of the valley dedicate songs to that fog, the rosy haze that sways over the waters of the great rivers that moisten it. They consider it a blessing. There is a very rhythmic dance in which girls dressed in festive costumes, with their cheerful aprons and empty amphorae, mimic the ceremony of drawing water from the river. And upon the river, boats glide and layers of pearly clouds hover, while everything around it seems to be life itself and graceful movement.

With her heart pounding, Kohar remembers the great hall where she led the river dance last year, and how they had decorated it, and how beautiful the shimmering ribbon of silver-colored water was, and the boat that moved upstage! And how she had laughed with the other girls when the apparatus that moved the boat jammed and the boy who was peddling from below stage suddenly popped up his head giggling and stopped the whole show! She liked him, Avedis, a lot. But who knows where Avedis is today; who knows if he is alive . . .

The presence of danger provokes confusion and panic in some. It gives others that commanding lucidity that makes others obey them. Kohar, without a second thought, takes charge of the little group; and everyone else gratefully follows her.

She looks around. "First of all, let us go to the holy site of Surp Arakelots. There we can get a good idea of the situation. By now we are close, and the fire seems to be contained. I think it is impossible that the gigantic building complex—with its churches and chapels, immense columned hall, and cells and refectory—was completely destroyed. Most likely, it is not all burnt. We can take shelter there for a bit. There might even be some hidden supplies. Our people up in Sassoun will also need food, if we end up there. What's more, if they set the monastery on fire, that means that they had already sacked it, or at least whatever was left after the events of twenty years ago, and that it can't billet the soldiers. But they can't have destroyed everything. Let's walk carefully, and once we reach the edge of the woods, it would be best if only one of us goes on ahead."

These words, which were more like thoughts spoken out loud, seem sensible. Everyone nods. As Kohar begins to move, Makarios stops her. "I am Greek," he says. "I'll go."

Chapter Nine

When they look onto the grounds of the Holy Apostles, they all have visions of the strong walls and fortifications of that most ancient and venerated place, which had for centuries been a famous center of culture and the production of illuminated manuscripts. They expect to find some signs of life, traces of village inhabitants who have always sought shelter up there when in danger, near the great dome, under the protection of the majestic *khatchkars*, stone crosses that have accompanied the lives of Anatolian farmers for millennia.

Makarios goes ahead first. Cautiously, he looks around, then forcefully signals to the others. They walk bent over, in silence, trying not to make any noise, though they needn't have worried. They make their way past walls. There is no one in the great courtyard, only the steady wind that lifts Father Hilarion's habit, as he lies there dead, with a crushed skull in front of the church door, and with a curiously peaceful and gentle air, his hand outstretched as though he had invited his murderer to enter the House of God. His face is calm and serene.

In the back, near the stairs to the upper floor, lies the abbot collapsed in a heap. He died too, but fighting: a long club lies broken at his feet, and an axe that softly rocks in the wind is stuck in his chest, like an evil, definitive banner of victory. The killer had not even retrieved it from the chest of the dead man; he had left it in him like a trophy and a warning to any passerby. The face of old *vartabed* Hovhannes is still twisted in his spasmodic attempt to die with honor defending his church; but the windows of the bell tower are shattered, and the magnificent walnut door with its thousands of inlays lies on the ground, covered in dust and blood. Hovering over everything is the acrid smell of the fire, which has since died down, a cloying mix of tar, wax, and burnt cloth that pierces noses and hearts, making it difficult both to cry and to breathe.

The little group of five moves together scared and guarded, looking about, peering at the corners of the large atrium in ruins, in the cells of the monks upstairs, and in the refectory. There is truly no one there. And that means that no one from the village managed to escape, that Anoush and Kohar had, the night before, crossed the land of the dead alive, and that the dead included the entire village, even Anoush's husband and children, and Kohar's fiancé.

Anoush walks in the deserted monastery. With every step the weight on her shoulders grows immense, and her hands intertwine in a desperate attempt to say an impossible prayer. Her lips closed, she mumbles a lullaby, clasping her hands ever more tightly. The others follow her in silence, until Eleni lengthens her stride, grabs her arm, and comforts her in a consoling embrace.

Eleni sits on the ground, pulling Anoush onto her lap, and begins to rock her slowly. On the other side, Hovsep takes Anoush's hands and places them on his heart. They all stop, waiting, fearing what they will discover, yet eager to know it, to put uncertainty behind them.

The others stand there, still, around the two women on the ground. A frail flame of hope still burns in each of those shy hearts—one never knows. Armenians have a thousand lives, how else could they have survived under their subjugators, century after century, and still held on to their language and customs? It is Hovsep who discovers something, following his nose: the chicken coop. He had picked up the faint scent of the birds, mingled with something dark: blood. Just so, right around the corner, in a small isolated shack that was in bad shape but still standing, they find a rooster and a pair of hens, huddled together silently in front of the body of a third monk, the good Father Tateos, who had grabbed the door and fallen askew, leaving his habit raised and his gnarled feet exposed.

There were only three monks left at Saint Arakelots, and they had killed them all. There is no one left at the monastery, and they all feel the weight of total abandonment, an apocalyptic dream, the end of their world.

But the chicken coop stands in front of them, and their hunger awakens.

Eleni starts chasing a big fat hen and sends Hovsep off to gather some wood; there is no shortage of it around. Makarios and Kohar, on the other hand, care for the dead. They drag the three bodies outside, one after the other, and under a big tree dig a grave deep enough to house them all.

They bury the three monks with their feet pointed east, as is customary, and place one cross—two branches hastily tied together—in each of their crossed hands. "They will wait for judgment day together, just as they lived together," Makarios says gravely. "But let us put the abbot, who is the most important of them, on top." Before shoveling the dirt, Kohar kneels down, diligently cleans the abbot's face with a wet cloth, and patiently straightens him. "He looked too angry," she says. "He could not present himself to the Supreme Court like that."

Makarios does not respond. He concentrates on shoveling energetically. Then they both level the ground with meticulous care. With the sharpened instincts of the persecuted, they realize this must be a hidden tomb, known only to God, who always sees where His servants are. Any distinctive marker would result in profanation and savage vandalism, in that anxious and spasmodic search for valuables and jewelry—the legendary "hidden gold of the Armenians"—of which still today the shepherds dream in far eastern Anatolia.

They return to the others like two hungry laborers. The chicken is almost roasted. Hovsep had found the monk's garden, and he gathered a few cucumbers and some beautiful yellow apricots. Thus they eat, in that blinding silence, seated near each other on the stone bench. The silent angel is with them.

Chapter Ten

Having picked the last little bone clean (even Anoush had ever so slowly eaten something), they all look at each other questioningly. In the end, deathly exhaustion and uncertainty prevail, and without saying much, the five of them settle in two corner cells upstairs that are still standing and are protected by an immense poplar tree, the presence of which mysteriously consoles them. Hovsep thinks that if the bad men return, he can escape on the tree and maybe take Anoush with him. He has appointed himself guardian of this desperate mother who had lost her little ones, and he asks himself, deep down in his orphan heart, if she will ever be able to accept him as a surrogate son. *Her smell is different from my mom's*, he thinks. *But it is still a mom smell, warm and sweet. I don't want to lose this one. I will take care of her.*

The next day is a beautiful one, with light clouds and a fresh breeze that is unusual for the season. Everyone awakes feeling a bit restored. Kohar finds Father

Hilarion's big broom still intact in a corner untouched by the flames and starts energetically sweeping the pavement of the great courtyard. Then she draws some water and puts it on to boil. Eleni had found a bunch of very aromatic mountain sage. They will make a tea of sorts to drink with the big loaf of bread, which Eleni grabs from Anoush's bag. Makarios, the skeptical and wandering Greek, the only man in the group, gets up, says the blessing of the *pater familias,* and carefully breaks the loaf. They cannot waste any of it, not even a crumb. Who knows where they will find more bread?

Soon they begin to talk. Anoush and Kohar want to go east, reach the border and cross it, somehow. The Russians are on the other side. There they will be safe. After the massacres of 1894 to 1896, how many people from their village—especially those who had dared to protest, to make themselves heard—had escaped toward the Caucasus? In the many gorges up there, deserters and outlaws can survive a long time. They become shepherds and goatherds. All they have to do is go with their heads held high to a clan chieftain, and be loyal and work hard.

Others had emigrated to the big cities in the Empire or farther away, to the west and even to the United States, to lead miserable, meager lives with the dream of being able to send some help to their families back home. These people are called *pandukhts,* and they live everywhere, in ports and in the suburbs, in Smyrna, Constantinople, Aleppo; they are servants, porters, drudges.

44

The two Greeks, on the other hand, are thinking of joining their compatriots, the *Rumi*, on the Ionian coast and, therefore, want to head west. Little Hovsep does not vote. He just clings to Anoush's skirt.

At some point, though, he gets tired of sitting still and runs off toward the chicken coop, which is now, sadly, almost empty. After they had killed the monks, and before setting the monastery on fire, the hungry soldiers had taken care of the chickens. They had caught nearly all of them. But the rooster was left unharmed, and he struts haughtily, as though he had had fifty chickens behind him. The fascinated child follows it to a small inside room, cluttered with broken baskets. A rake leans unsteadily against the wall. Hovsep disappears from sight.

Eleni is distracted as she watches the boy. She does not have children; she brings other people's children into the world. She is respected and capable, and during a birth knows how to make decisions and give orders. But yesterday she rediscovered Makarios and feels more fragile and womanly, so her eyes follow Hovsep, that precious lucky charm, the boy who knew how to keep quiet and save his life while his family died. She sees him disappear into the darkness and, after a bit, grows anxious. While the others continue to argue without getting anywhere, she stands up and walks toward the dark storeroom.

There, in the back, is a brooding hen. Standing still in front of it, Hovsep contemplates the bird and her sovereign tranquility. Eleni is very happy at the discovery; it somehow comforts her, this scene of life hatching in the midst of the horror of fire and massacre. But her sharp eyes catch a glimmer in the back, behind the brooding hen, in the darkest corner of the room.

Walking slowly, so as not to disturb the brood, she goes back to see. There really is something on the ground, a flat and rectangular form, from which brilliant colors transpire, here and there, like jewels. Some straw has been hastily scattered on top of it, but the job is clearly incomplete. Eleni has a mental flash: Is that what the the rake leaning against the wall was for? The body of the old monk, Tateos, lay there right in front of it. Maybe he had tried to divert attention from something that he had hidden in the back.

Feverishly, she begins to brush the straw away. She uncovers a scene filled with the vivid and festive colors of the sky, the sun, and the grass of Anatolian summers. Also in the scene are a city in the background, trees, and figures: it is Christ entering Jerusalem on a donkey. It is an illuminated manuscript, huge in size. It must have opened when it fell on the ground. Poor Tateos, who was fleeing, did not even have the time to close it, as heavy as it is. He just threw some straw on it and went to the door to defend the book with his body.

He died, but his treasure remained safe. Eleni lays her rough hands on the parchment and slowly caresses it. She has already understood what it is: it is the treasure of Surp Arakelots Monastery, the famous *Msho*

Charantir, the "Book of Sermons" of Moush. The Armenians believe this ancient illuminated manuscript is the largest of its kind in the world, measuring about three feet long, and a foot and a half wide. It weighs about sixty pounds, as everyone repeats with proud admiration, and everyone in the valley believes that it has thaumaturgic powers. The abbot and two monks would solemnly carry it to the sick in a profluvium of incense. [1]

Eleni does not know much about manuscripts, even though maestro Manuel, who was so proud of his exotic name, would tell her stories on their Sunday afternoon walks in the park about the heroic monks who would copy the books of their ancient forefathers, shut off in their monasteries on the mountains, and add *colophons*—accounts of their own times—in the margins. These *colophons* would tell of kings, princes, and the people, of wars and invasions that devastated the land, written in minute script. "War after war, conquest after conquest," the maestro used to say passionately, "those humble and wise monks described the issues of our people, who were always dominated by a foreign power, but always remained faithful to their language and to the Cross."

---

1   Composed between 1200 and 1202, the *Msho Charantir* (The Homiliary of Moush) is a collection of homilies copied in the *scriptorum* of the Avakvank Monastery near Erzynka. It was commissioned by a devout merchant who had it illuminated in splendid miniatures. During the Mongol invasion of 1203, the merchant was killed, and the book was stolen. Hearing that the lost precious manuscript was being sold a few years later, the monks of the Monastery of the Holy Apostles of Moush bought it at a very high price after difficult negotiations, and they protected the precious relic at their monastery for centuries.

She had never seen the Book of Moush up close, only from afar amid spirals of incense and chanting monks, in some procession when it was displayed for the people to admire and venerate. And now it lies there on the ground, in the storeroom, behind the hen that continues to brood peacefully. For a moment, Eleni lets herself think of keeping it. Perhaps, she thinks, it will bring her luck in the uncertain future that lies before her. With the flaps of her apron, she delicately cleans it, and the colors gleam and captivate. Eleni feels blessed and happy, contemplating those immobile figures that were filled with life, those illuminated capitals, the delicately interlaced decorations that seem, like enchanted animals, to flash along the margins of the pages, and the Armenian letters that stretch one after the other like a mysterious embroidery.

She speaks that guttural and sweet language quite well, but does not know its alphabet. She never needed to. She looks at it as if it were a musical score, with its numinous letters that rise and fall on the lines, and she seems to hear the solemn chants of the rituals, the deep voices of the men who ask for God's forgiveness.

Eleni takes off her apron, uses it to clean the open page a bit, then carefully closes the sacred book. A cloud of dust rises, she coughs, and this upsets the brooding hen, who begins furiously to flap her wings.

Chapter Eleven

At that moment, Eleni hears a patter behind her. It is Hovsep, who has snapped out from under the spell and cautiously bends over the agitated hen that is frenetically fretting. He wants to take an egg and does not give a whit that it is almost ready to hatch. He is hungry, and there is food there. It is simple.

Eleni, who was about to stop his hand, holds back. If there is no more future, no more hope in that land, for her and Makarios, who are Greeks and foreigners, then what kind of fate is being woven for a child of that damned race? How long can he survive on his own? He is marked for death. What difference does it make if he takes an egg and ruins the brood? Surely, they had taught him not to disturb mothers: the cow with her calf, the hen, the goat. But his ordered childhood world has gone to pieces. His mother did not defend him. She abandoned him, without a word, sinking in blood.

She had left him, and he was betrayed. He had to hide in the dark, plunge in the dark. Now he knows that parents do not protect their children. His sister is also dead. Only he managed to save his life. Henceforth, Hovsep will know how to take care of himself and will have only one goal: to take care of Anoush, who is weaker than he. He will protect her, following her, watching over her. He only wanted to be able to lie beside her at night and watch her sleep so that he can every so often breathe in her smell of a mother. He will develop a fierce combination of caution and cunning to guide her toward salvation.

Eleni understands, so she lets him be. With great effort, she lifts the heavy book and makes her way toward the others.

She finds them still discussing the direction of their escape. But now there is another heavy matter, quite literally: What to do with the Book of Moush? It is not just ancient and precious; it is proof, a reality, a wonder. They all stand up, overcome and awe-struck. Every hand reaches out, hesitant, to touch it. What to do with it? The thing had crossed seven centuries: a symbol of a civilization and a pledge of devotion, a veneration of the words of the ancients and of the images painted in the illuminations, the survivor of a culture and a world that was now disappearing in the fire and flames of senseless destruction.

Again the question remains: How to protect it, this sign of salvation? It is not a jewel; it is not gold; it is not coins. One can always bury a treasure. In these ill-fated days many Armenians attempt to do just that, digging holes in their gardens, moving bricks in their homes. Paltry cunning, quickly detected. It is impossible to hide the Book of Moush. It is too big. What is more, they all consider its discovery as a sign from God. "The book will save us," says Kohar, visibly moved. "We must take it with us."

"Silly woman," Makarios responds impatiently. He is tired of the discussions that have delayed his escape. His was the right idea, and he does not feel like splitting hairs with these bewildered people. At this point, he just wants to leave.

But Eleni, an attentive guardian, holds the heavy bundle with both of her hands. She seems superstitiously convinced that the book will be a talisman for all of them, and that they must stick together. There is a reason why it has come into their hands. It means that the angels who watched over it decided to give it not to wise priests who touched it "with immaculate hands," as the liturgy proclaims, but expressly to them, this small company of three women, a boy, and a man, fleeing toward the mountains, and united by chance among the ruins of the monastery.

"The book will come with us. We will take turns carrying it," Kohar says. "But first of all let us all swear that we will protect it with our lives, from any insult or profanation." They all solemnly swear, even Makarios, who, however, prudently crosses his fingers behind his back. They then make sage tea, sit down in a circle, and begin to turn one page after the other, enchanted by the magnificent writing and iridescent illuminated capitals.

Even Hovsep, back from his visit to the brooding hen, timidly reaches out with a little egg-stained hand, leaving a long streak of egg white on the gold of an illuminated page. The stain looks like a tear. The image is of the Mother of God, who seems to be asleep under a red and blue sky, surrounded by adoring angels. It is then, as he touches the beautiful face of the sleeping woman who looks so much like the mother he left behind lying in her own blood, that Hovsep feels the tears of consolation watering his heart, giving him the courage to believe that he will be able to survive.

Chapter Twelve

"It is best," counsels Makarios, "to wait for nightfall to leave." He has given up his hope of immediate departure. "But we must find another lantern and some supplies."

Hovsep and Anoush start searching in all the corners. It takes patience, and they both have a lot of that. Meanwhile, Eleni and Kohar get organized. They had found two big, sturdy baskets, which they fill up with everything they find in the most remote rooms behind the woodpile, where they know monks often hide food for times of want. But the pickings are scarce. The soldiers had thoroughly rummaged before starting the fire.

In a cellar devastated by the fire, under fallen beams, they finally and luckily discover a small treasure of apples, apricots, plums, walnuts, and hazelnuts left to dry. The fire had only barely roasted them once the strings on which the fruit had hung were burnt. "It's good stuff, and gives energy," Kohar says gravely, piling up the loot. "We must take things that won't spoil."

Eleni responds with a smile and fills up her apron. "Well, water won't be a problem. The valley of Moush is full of springs," she adds. But then she remembers that they will have to climb up toward the high mountain of Sassoun, where she had never been. "The springs," she thinks a bit anxiously, "will surely be fewer on the mountain. But what can we do?"

"I know where there's water," Kohar responds, grasping the other woman's fear. "I've climbed up there many times." She points to a crag far off in the horizon, where the proud Armenians of Sassoun have defended their independence for centuries.

In a large chest, they find a pair of old habits. They are dirty and ugly, but they are made of heavy wool and can be used as blankets. They also find an antique copper pitcher that is dented, but exquisitely decorated with garlands and clusters of fruit and leaves. Kohar looks at it uncertainly and ties it with a string to the top of the basket, which she lifts on her shoulders. Eleni laughs out loud, guessing that Kohar is taking it because she likes it, because she has nothing from her home, because she has lost everything, even her most precious things. The truth is that only Eleni and Makarios were able to do some packing, to bring some mementos of their former lives. But no one, on that day of somber sadness, dares to foresee the future.

Makarios, meanwhile, finds a storeroom that has some pipe tobacco. But where are the pipes? In the end, he forces himself to think like an old monk who occasionally indulges in that modest pleasure. It must have been at the end of the day, in the evening, when it was getting dark in the large convent kitchen. And it is indeed there that he discovers two shabby pipes in the corner of the chimney, hidden under a brick that had protected them from the fire.

Inside the more battered pipe, which was full of cobwebs, he hears the clinking of coins. It is two gold florins, carefully wrapped in a cloth, and a few ancient silver coins. He polishes one of them and sees the face of Ardashes, the great king who wanted to give the kingdom of Armenia a seat worthy of his ambition. He designed his wonderous capital, Artashat (*Artaxata*, in his native tongue), with the help of Hannibal the Carthaginian, who was exiled after his defeat at Zama. "Who knows where old Hilarion found those coins," Makarios says to himself, slipping them into his pocket. "Certainly, they were of no service to him. But I'll know how to make good use of them,"

At that moment, Hovsep returns triumphant, pulling the silent Anoush with him. He had found two lanterns, and one of them is in good shape and can be used right away. The other needs to be thoroughly cleaned to see if it can work. He also recovered a piece of flint, some candles, and even a braid of *bastegh* (dried grape paste) in a corner on the ground. He doesn't know how long the *bastegh* had been lying there, but he does not mention this last part. It will be part of his own little private reserve if things do not go well.

Every person in the company tries to keep something on the side and does not share it with the others, just as no member of the company reveals his or her deepest fears. The nightmares that torment them must remain secret: the future that waits for them is frightening enough.

Chapter Thirteen

Evening has fallen. They have all eaten, but the big problem rears its ugly face. Everyone had thought about it, and deep inside they hoped that Makarios, who, like all Greeks, is shrewd, would solve it. How are they to transport the book? There are no more animals at the monastery. Abbot Hovhannes's calm mare has disappeared, as have the two strong mules. All around them, in that vast desolated land, there is no one left.

Who can carry the book on his shoulders alone, during the unmeasurable time of their escape, of their being in hiding? How can they keep it from being recognized or stolen?

For a moment, Kohar thinks of building a sled of sorts: there is plenty wood for it, but building it takes time, and, besides, who would pull the sled? They are stuck standing in front of that magnificent ancient inheritance and can do nothing. *We are like the legendary king*, Anoush suddenly thinks, distracting herself from her nightmares, *imprisoned in his secret treasure chamber in the midst of the gleaming chests filled with jewels, but without bread and water.*

To die like that ... Anoush thinks, picturing the shimmering lights bouncing off the precious stones and the door barred shut. *But at least no one can strip and rape you.* She shudders, her mind filled with dark forebodings. While they all look at each other with worry, it is Hovsep who comes up with an idea: "Let's divide this enormous book. It's too big. Let's cut it into many pieces, and each of us can carry it."

The idea seems insane, but Hovsep convinces them. It is, after all, the only possible solution. "Besides," Eleni adds, "if any one of us is caught and killed, we will at least not lose the whole book." At this point Kohar suggests a variant on the plan: "The Book of Moush is too precious for us to cut it up into five pieces. Many internal pages will be ruined by the sun, sweat, and even rain. Let's divide it into two parts, and Anoush and I will carry it."

Hovsep is very offended that he is not considered up to the task, but quickly gives in. He will always stay close to Anoush and will help her carry her part of the weight whenever she gets tired. He is the guardian of Anoush and hence also of half the book.

It was thus that those five derelicts prepared the incredible rescue. They quickly find a large knife in the kitchen, and Makarios carefully tests the sharpness of the blade. Next, they place the book on the huge oak table in the abandoned refectory, after giving it a thorough cleaning. The women gently pass soft rags over the illuminations and the elegant letters of the Armenian alphabet that chase each other harmoniously page after page. They run through the entire book, dusting each page with the greatest of care. Then they lay open the book in the exact middle, and it is then, and only then, that Makarios wields the knife.

He slowly cuts through the thick spine, which had been reinforced with wooden splints, starting from the top. Fine dust falls lightly to the floor, and Hovsep quickly runs to touch it. It looks like flour, or a light intangible powder. The intense and arid smell of well-preserved old manuscripts is unleashed from the ancient pages. It is intoxicating. They all come close to the book and breathe it in with unrestrained pleasure.

As the knife slowly advances, they all fear that they are doing something sacrilegious. Kohar and Anoush cross themselves profusely, to steel themselves. No one intervenes to stop the Greek, who is working with extreme concentration. "How many skins of one-month-old calves did they need for these enormous pages?" he asks himself idly, as he focuses on the tip of the blade. "There are so many of them." The adventurous history of the precious manuscript floods his mind. It had been stolen, found, and repurchased by the monks. *Seven-hundred years!* Makarios thinks. *And it is still so beautiful. It must be worth a fortune.*

It is finally done. Makarios straightens his back and puts away the knife. The women hasten to clean the two halves again. Even divided, each part is still enormous and very heavy. They wrap each part with the most precious cloth that they could find: a ceremonial vestment of embroidered silk, which they had cut in half without regret. Then they try to load it onto their shoulders.

The weight, however, is still too great for them. So with some small wooden boards, the crafty Greek builds a frame of sorts that distributes the load more evenly across the back. With some leather cords that he had found in the stables, he firmly ties the boards together, and secures them in front. They had ransacked everything and had taken the animals, but Makarios thought he could still find a thing or two in the corners of the stalls, even after the fire. And he did. There were leather cords, wooden boards, nails, and an assortment of other useful things.

It is now night. The slow twilight has given in to a velvety, inviting darkness. The last hen and rooster have been devoured. A flask of wine completed their dinner. They need to move on. Anoush and Kohar ready themselves. They place a blanket between the wooden frame and their shoulders, and arm themselves with strong staffs. They tie some food, a flask for water, and a knife to their belts. They are ready. They look around defiantly. Hovsep then also grabs a stick, the largest he can manage, and starts off behind them. The last two are Eleni and Makarios, laden with their bags. And thus on that starry night, illuminated by a pale moon, they all move, each thinking of the past, each fearing the future.

Chapter Fourteen

Their direction is in the end forced upon them, slowed as they are by the two women and the book. They head south for the impregnable massif of Sassoun. There, according to legend, the great princely families defended their independence for centuries. There, last century, the Armenians defended themselves with honor. There, the great Antranik hailed from, the man with no fear, the one who always fought like a lion, who a few years ago had barricaded himself and his men behind the monastery walls of Saint Arakelots to break out of a siege with the subtle cunning of mountain folk.

There are only a few heroic deeds in the last few centuries of which the Armenian people can boast. After the fall of the kingdom and its splendid capital, Ani, the city of a thousand and one churches, squeezed by the great bordering empires—the Byzantines and the advancing Seljuk Turks—the people survived by bowing their heads, tying themselves to the land and to the work of its artisans and merchants, dotting the

61

country with churches, stone crosses, and monasteries. The monastaries housed legions of skilled monks who transcribed, translated, and illuminated stupendous manuscripts with wise hands, and in these sacred places schools of the great masters of the exquisite art of the miniature flourished.

Today, no one knows how many manuscripts were destroyed in that terrible summer of fire in 1915, a summer that went up in smoke with the naïve souls of the farmers of the Armenian valleys. The churches, the homes, the stone crosses took a little longer to disappear, but today their presence has been completely erased in eastern Anatolia. One can still, perhaps, catch a glimpse of it in the restless ghosts who populate the fogs of Moush, and who show themselves only to the eyes of merciful wayfarers.

But in that warm night of June, the little group of five fugitives does not think about such things. They put one foot in front of the other, as silently as possible, and the heavy breathing of the two women bent under a great weight accompanies them like a rhythmic under-current. The earth on the path is soft, and being in a group consoles them.

In the end, they arrive at the fortress of the steep massif of Sassoun. And there, they finally learn the truth. Camped all around are the few survivors of the great massacre: the men who were in the high pastures, a woman here and there doing the wash in a secluded riverbend, a few children with wide eyes. The cripple

Aram moves from one group of people to the next, with a mournful face, bearing horrendous news. He had hidden inside an oven that was still warm. No one had thought of searching the oven. The freshly made bread was already on the table, and the soldiers sat down and had greedily shared it.

That is how the five from the monastery come to know the details of the massacres of Moush. Blood ran black in the streets of the city and the hundreds of villages in the valley. Barns and haylofts were used to eliminate the women and children. It was a planned and precise elimination, a scientific one, to empty the valley of all Armenian blood, which the earth would drink and, by doing so, become more fertile.

A blanket of abject fear floats suspended over the people, like the thickest fog, and blunts their hearts and thoughts. *What to do now?* they ask themselves, because Sassoun is surely unconquerable (or at least that is the hope), but it cannot provide everyone with shelter or, above all, with food. And the *Moushetsi*, who are much richer than their relatives in the mountains, had been improvident and incautious. They have no supplies with them. "They only know how to flee, these weaklings," whisper the proud people of the crag. "They have brought no food, or weapons."

"But they still are our blood brothers," says Arzuman, the exile who has returned to fight with his brothers. "We can't leave them in the hands of the murderers, who will certainly come looking for them."

His words hold weight. Thus reluctantly, the *Sassountsi* open the gates and give shelter to them all, including the group from the monastery. The five of them stand united and try to hide the bulky packages carried by the two women.

Chapter Fifteen

In the following days, life becomes difficult for the refugees in Sassoun. Orders issued from the capital concerning the Armenians were peremptory, and the army has decided to finish the job, to put an end to that arrogant bunch of Armenians clinging to the mountain and refusing to play the role of defenseless victim. "Sassoun has always been a problem," the commanding colonel tells his troops. "Let's try to make quick work of it. It is indecent that they are able to resist. It won't take long to overcome them."

Refreshed from the fatigue and tension of the front lines, thanks to the food found in the villages and the days of indolence and peaceful slumber, the soldiers and officers applaud enthusiastically. What riches have these greedy and rich Armenians hidden in their mountain villages that were never conquered by the sultan's troops? How many jewels, how many precious stones, how many bags of gold coins are safeguarded by those ancient caves carved in the rock? The humiliated hearts of those poor farmers, forced into the army, unused to harsh military discipline, and punished for trifles, quiver at the idea that there are people even less fortunate than they who have rebelled against the power of the Empire, vile traitors who have made deals with the detested Europeans so that they can subjugate and ridicule the honest subjects of the Star and Crescent Moon.

It is a *jihad*, a holy war, to them. It happens also to help them fill their pockets a bit. Rows of camels laden with plundered treasure from the deserted homes of the Armenians are leaving the valley of Moush; the colonel has already set himself up like a *pasha* in the beautiful residence of Dr. Rupen Aboyan, a physician and influential member of the community, who was among the first to be killed. He tastes the succulent peaches of the orchard with pleasure, smokes the good doctor's pipes, and had immediately ordered the three beautiful carpets from Mrs. Aboyan's sitting room and her delicate Viennese porcelain to be wrapped up and sent to his home in Constantinople.

He has kept one of their daughters as a servant, but the girl does not give him much satisfaction. He is already thinking of passing her on to the troops. Nevertheless, he has decided to be patient for the moment. She is quite pretty and might just need to be tamed. She is wild and scratches him when they are alone. He likes this. But she cries too much, and that is something he cannot stand. He will have his wife, Fethiyé, join him. She is good at creating a comfortable environment for him, and at breaking in women; she will know how to make a perfect maid out of the handsome girl.

The good colonel sighs and looks absentmindedly at the lawn in front of the house. There, on the left, he sees a leafy copse overlaid with the climbing roses that his wife loves so much; on the right, he sees a sheltered bench shaded by a multicolored awning, the coffee cart at hand. His daydreaming is interrupted by a young, breathless officer, a messenger bearing bad news of the desperate resistance of the Armenians of Sassoun, who have decided to die rather than surrender. "We either die here now, or later in your hands," a disheveled boy had yelled from the top of a massive wall. "We have no choice. We all have to die, but at least not alone." The boy had spat with contempt, and the women behind him had cried out mournfully. They had repeated the names of slaughtered loved ones over and over; then every few minutes, they would stop, look at each other, and would let out a powerful, blood-curdling wail.

The Turkish soldiers below had begun to feel uneasy. It is one thing to kill in battle, or to surprise an unarmed enemy in his sleep; it is quite another to hear all those names chanted by strident, hate-filled voices that penetrate the ears and perforate the skull. They had sent Lieutenant Ahmed, who is young and courageous, to speak to the colonel. Like them, Ahmed is shaken by the wild cries of the women, and had covered his ears.

But the colonel has no change of mind. He is a career soldier and has been at it for some time. He knows that the rebels uptop the mountain do not have much food and cannot get any. He dismisses the lieutenant with a wave and sends him back to the camp. "The envious are everywhere," he sighs, "and I do not want slander or the suspicion of insufficient zeal to be associated with my name." He is a personal friend of the minister of war, Enver, and knows well that the sooner the Armenian matter is taken care of, the better.

Meanwhile in Sassoun, food is in short supply. Abandoned children grown wild rummage all over the place and steal anything that looks edible. There are no more cats to be seen, and the hunt for mice has begun. Water is running out.

Chapter Sixteen

Kohar and her group have always been at each other's
sides. They have shared food and water, and only rarely
stepped away from their corner. Each night they sleep
near each other, and during the day one of them always
guards the worn-out blanket that protects their pallet.
They divvied up chores without complaint. At times,
Makarios, conscious of being the only non-Armenian
male within that grave and desperate community, goes
out snooping. Protecting the book has become a sacred
duty for them all: they have dedicated their lives to it
and think of nothing else.

One of the other refugees has begun to look at them
with suspicion. They are the only survivors of their village. Why? What are those five motley people hiding
so jealously under that blanket? "Surely it is something
precious," Yeghisapet, wife to the cobbler Varto, tells
the other women. She had watched her husband and
their four sons burn alive in a barn with the other men
from her village, and hears their screams replay every
night, waking up with screams of her own.

She goes around all day, with her haunted and wicked eyes, muttering to herself and spitting out curses. The other women fear and avoid her. Some, who have had the good fortune of saving one or two of their children, pull them close and lower their gazes when she passes by. But in the evening of their fourth day, it began to rain hard upon the miserable crowd. Thunder and lightening chase each other. "It is as if the Almighty Himself is tired of us, and wants to kick us out," whispers little Lilia. Named after a flower, she is the daughter of a shirtmaker who knows how to make corsets, flowery blouses, and embroidered party aprons like no other.

Suddenly, Yeghisapet gets up and makes for Kohar, who is sitting straight while the others try to sleep. "You over there, who are you really?" she shouts. "What are you hiding under there?" She springs, grabbing Kohar by the hair and violently shaking her. Kohar reacts calmly, grabs the widow's hands, and pushes her to the ground without saying a word. Then she stands up and places her hands on her hips, glaring at her attacker.

The other woman pulls back but is no longer alone. Other women have approached and watch the scene with an angry fixedness, drawn to it, as though being part of a herd and attacking someone might lessen the fear and horror of the moment. Then from farther back, a man comes forth, one of the fighters. "What's the matter, women? Can't you sleep?" Then he too begins to stare at Kohar, who is still standing in her belligerent pose. "What are you hiding back there?" he questions her. "Look here, all food needs to be shared. You cannot keep it for yourselves! For now, return to where you were, but we'll check tomorrow."

Kohar sits back down and shudders. There is no question: tomorrow they will have to show what they are hiding. She knows that the very sight of the Book of Moush in their hands will stir up a hornet's nest. Everyone in the valley knows that book. Everyone knows that it is the most precious treasure of the Holy Apostles Monastery. They have all climbed to the sanctuary on one festivity or another. They are all proud of that wonderous reality that reminds them of the glory and splendor of their ancestors. They all admire the monastery's carved doors and illuminated manuscripts. They do not understand a word of the book, but they can contemplate the illustrations: the beautiful images of saints, scenes from the Gospel, the rapt and pious expression of the Virgin, Christ Pantocrator watching from above.

Not one of these oppressed and offended survivors, who are scared to death, will readily accept that this company dared to touch the sacred book, and to sacrilegiously cut it in half. They will think that they tried to steal it, that they are hiding it to smuggle it to Russia and sell it. They will not believe their explanations, of this Kohar is sure. So what to do now?

They need to leave; they need to escape, to get away fast before the encircling of Sassoun is complete, before real hunger sets in. Kohar understands this with blinding clarity, just as she understands that the only

71

possible direction for their escape is east, toward the Russian outposts, in the hopes of crossing paths with the advancing czarists. But she also knows that attempting a getaway on one's own is a terrible risk: there are stragglers, deserters, and *cheté*—the killing squads, the so-called Special Organization—not to mention normal gendarmes, lurking everywhere to flush out the surviving Armenians.

Just then, Eleni joins her. The Greek woman is uneasy; her nomadic instincts have warned her that the provisional refuge of Sassoun is not safe. In her sleep came an omen, a sign. The winds of the islands had reached her in a dream. The *meltemi* was blowing, an ominous and strange storm, and her mother appeared before her with a hawthorn branch in her hand, pointing at the way. Makarios was not in the dream. Nor were the others. It was only her, in a dark dress battered by the wind, and her mother, Elektra, clad in white with the branch in her hand. Eleni had smelled the scent of the hawthorn and of myrtle carried by the wind. Then her mother effortlessly picked up the Book of Moush with one hand and gave it to her with a nod as if to say, "Go, child. That is your path. Make no mistakes this time. The silent angel is with you." At that, a beautiful young angel with enormous wings inlaid with the thousand colors of the miniature really does materialize behind her shoulders.

Chapter Seventeen

Kohar and Eleni look at each other, and at that moment they become sisters. The strength of the one will become the strength of the other, and, together, they will see to Anoush, the absentminded Makarios, and little Hovsep. They had both received the message, and they begin to speak in brisk whispers, preparing their escape.

"We need to get away from here, from this mortal trap," whispers Kohar, who recounts what had happened with poor Yeghisapet. "And we have to do it tonight."

"Let's wake the others in a bit," says Eleni. "But meanwhile, we have to decide how to flee."

They don't have to walk far to leave the place. The village where the refugees settled has streets and houses that grew without any particular order. They were built close to each other and with a surrounding wall to protect the inhabitants from the endless forays of their aggressive neighbors. From the corner of the empty barn where they are camped out, Kohar and her group can leave in a snap, but they have to do so without attracting attention. Above all, they have to get the book out without raising more questions.

They wake Makarios first. Explaining the situation to him is not easy. He is nervous and disheveled; he yawns and complains. Eleni puts her hand to his mouth and presses down firmly. She whispers Yeghisapet's threats in his ear and tells him why it is necessary to escape from her morbid curiosity and that of the other women. He surrenders, as he too had noticed the inquisitive looks.

As for Anoush and Hovsep, all it took was getting them to move. He needs to go where she goes, and she always follows Kohar closely, as though the girl were the living portal that separates her from the unbearable reality nested in her memory.

Thus they slowly and quietly drag their feet like people who are unable to sleep and have to make their way between others who are fast asleep. They send Anoush and the little boy ahead. As soon as the two are out of sight, it is Makarios's turn. He pretends to go out to grab a smoke with the sleepless men. Finally, it is the turn of Kohar and Eleni. They gather their things with feigned nonchalance and wrap the two halves of the book more tightly with the bit of leftover food they have. Then, in the darkest corner, they tie the bronze pot and cups they received from the village women to their waists, and calmly walk toward the exit on the high road, the one that leads out of the village and up toward the mountains. It is not really a road, but rather a goat trail that is difficult to take even in daylight.

But they have no choice. They all meet up in the dark of the cool summer night and take each other by the hand. They make up a small chain of hands that squeeze each other nervously, trying to stay close, to transmit warmth, courage.

They are headed east. In the beginning, they walk quickly, breathing in lungfuls of the crisp mountain air that is so pleasant after the foul air of the barn. Once they are far enough, Kohar lights the lantern and leads the march, trying to dim its tenuous light with her hand. Everyone is quiet—each of them immersed in thought. The silent angel accompanies them.

What is the best advice for his charges: save your lives or save the book? How would they feel if they lost the book, that unique and precious evidence that the Armenians who are being sent to their destruction are not a mass of forlorn people, easy prey of an extermination campaign whose bewildered survivors will wander starving through the Mesopotamian plains, but the heirs of an ancient culture with extraordinary artistic traditions, who speak a complex and sophisticated language, and write in a venerable and elegant alphabet? Their churches are the fruits of crystalline architectural wisdom; their music and their dances move and captivate. But who would speak of the Armenians when the massacre is complete, if nothing and no one were to survive, without a trace of what they accomplished throughout the centuries?

These five people are in the care of the silent angel. It is for their own souls, the angel knows well, that saving the book is necessary. By saving the book they will save themselves. And thus with every step Makarios feels an affectionate kindness grow within him. It astonishes him but also fills his soul with joy. He feels himself becoming the father of that small people. It is he who will help them cross the fire of arid desolation and will lead them to safety beyond the mountains, beyond the anguish, beyond the horror. They will not sit and cry on the rivers of Babylon when they remember their lost land; they will have a new life, and it will be peaceful. Makarios the Greek has given his word. They have not yet completely escaped the net, but he is there and will provide for them.

Filled with cunning and new courage, Makarios no longer thinks about the Chora of Paros, about the idea that he had coddled, of returning there with Eleni and finally starting a family. "It is too late for me," he tells himself. "It's too late for everyone. But it's not too late to show them, those rabid dogs, that I am smarter than they are. Me, they always underestimated me, even the Armenians. But now they depend on me. I will save them, and I will lead them to the Caucasus. We will walk along Lake Van, cross the river. There are many shepherds there who don't really care about anything. All it will take is paying them, and they will help us cross the great mountain through the high paths that only they know."

It is late, and the night is getting darker and gloomier. They have been walking for an hour when the little one trips over a root and lets out a sharp squeak. He bravely tries to get back up on his feet, but can't, and begins silently to cry, terrified, clinging to Anoush's skirt. "Don't leave me here. I'll start walking right away," he cries. "Don't leave me." Such is his terror that with his other hand he grabs Eleni's foot, who also falls badly on Makarios. They all end up on the ground in a pile and begin to laugh uncontrollably.

Chapter Eighteen

That incredible, liberating laugh calms their nerves, making them all more serene—and more lucid. It makes no sense to continue walking in the dark, with the risk of ending up in the hands of some enemy patrol. What's more, they are tired. No one had really slept; they had been roused from their slumber and now feel the weight of harshly interrupted sleep.

They are free, in the open air. They had laughed heartily and with abandon, making a racket, but there was clearly no one around. And so, once they calm down, they stay seated on the ground and fall asleep, leaning on each other, breathing in the night air, listening to the muffled noises of the woods and far-off water. They have lost everything, but not themselves: like lighter shadows hovering over a shadow, here come their loved ones to console them, to cradle them in bodiless hands that are mysteriously present. From then on they will always be there, ready to welcome those who die and comfort those who resist. At long last, Kohar can be tender with her fiancé and tell him the sweet words that she used only to whisper in her heart.

At dawn, they look around. They are in a grove, and the water that they heard really is close by. It is a barely visible stream descending from the mountain. Even the path that they had followed seems to have disappeared. Standing up, Kohar realizes that there is a cliff not far ahead. They would have ended up on it had they continued on the night before. In a flash she understands, and is thankful. The night and their angels had protected and guided them. Their path was at best faint; no Turkish police patrol had heard them. They are now outside the encirclement, though most certainly not out of danger.

Everyone crowds around to see, rubbing their eyes. Afterward, communicating wordlessly, they go take a drink from the stream, eat a bit of bread, and begin to walk again. That entire day, they walk and walk, almost without stopping, and see no one except around noon, when they spot two shepherds far off on the mountain ahead. It's not clear if they are Kurds or Armenians. In doubt, they hide and steer clear of them. They climb and descend through valleys and slopes. No one speaks. They are focused on getting as far as possible from the cursed valley and the trap of the inhospitable massif of Sassoun.

They now understand many things. Their task is to save the book—even poor Yeghisapet's cries confirmed it. The book is their talisman. "Nothing will happen to us," Anoush suddenly chirps with the faint voice of a child, "if we walk through green pastures following the path prepared for us." Then, she sobs. "Nothing else can happen to me anymore. It is all finished . . ."

"I am not finished, Mom, *mayrig*," Hovsep says, hugging her tightly. "I am your son now. Come, let's go find some keepsake stones." He takes her by the hand, and they go off together looking at the ground, searching for little colored stones, which Hovsep carefully places in his haversack made out of pieces of old rugs. His mother had made it for him. It is the only thing he has left from his own family; it is his very own talisman. Eighty years later, in Glendale, California, after a long and industrious life as a laborer and painter, he will have it beside his pillow at the moment of his goodbye, that worn little sack, in which he had placed a handful of earth from his homeland before going into exile forever.

But on that summer day, it is the stones that interest him, and the nearness of poor Anoush's scent of a mother. She slowly seals the faces of her loved ones in the depths of her ailing heart. In caring for him, she rediscovers her wounded maternal instincts. During the long walk of their escape and exile, they will be inseparable. And so they will remain until the final chapter of their adventure when they are finally able to hand over the half of the book entrusted to them in Etchmiadzin Cathedral, the Holy Seat of the *katholikos* of all Armenians.

It will be then—once they have completed their mission—that they will be separated forever. Hovsep will be placed in a poor orphanage where young escapees from death will struggle to endure the cold and hunger of the harsh Caucasus winters. Most of them will end up in America. Anoush, on the other hand, will be sent to live with other single women who survived, bereft of loved ones. They will be photographed for an album published in Tbilisi in 1917: tragic, crushed derelicts with dazed expressions, who wander about feverishly, vainly searching for a bit of food and any other survivors from their villages. They stand straight in front of the photographer in all of their misery, prematurely aged and dressed in colorless rags, with bare feet and nervously wringing their hands. Adrift in their midst, all traces of Anoush will be lost.

Chapter Nineteen

In the evening of the first day of their march, spirits are quite high. They stop in a small meadow between two sun-parched hills in the shadow of a shady oak tree. They throw themselves to the ground. The grass is dewy and refreshes their tired legs. They do not want to get back up. They want to sleep right away, sink into the greenery.

But it is not possible. They need to eat something, check their scanty supplies, and refill their flasks with water. They have almost finished the bread. There are still a bit of cheese and some dried fruit left. "What if I try to catch a rabbit?" Makarios asks. "There are so many in these parts." But the idea is quickly discarded as they think of how to cook it. "Making a fire would be to announce ourselves with flags and tambourines," Eleni said, smiling.

Kohar finds some small dandelion hearts that are bitter but tasty, and she chews on them with a little piece of cheese. "We are not yet reduced to eating grass, like the poor women from Bitlis," she mutters, very softly, though, so that no one can hear her.

They sleep a little, huddled next to each other, and early the next morning are back on the road. And thus they go, day after day, through valleys and mountains, through screes and seemingly impassible paths—one day sighting a proud buck that ignores them—on and on, beset by hunger, with bloody feet and eyes blinded by the sun.

The women's handkerchiefs, tied tightly around their heads, are washed over and over, until their colors have completely faded. Hovsep's pants have huge holes, but he laughs as he pokes his fingers through them. Everyone's shoes have become shapeless and are held together by rags. Kohar blesses that providential intuition that led her to tie the three thick, large, pocket-filled aprons from her home around her waist.

The book is heavy and strains Kohar's and Anoush's tired shoulders. At times, they want to put it down, hide it somewhere, get rid of it. But Eleni is watchful, and she and Makarios take over for them. They load the two heavy bundles on their shoulders and walk with gritted teeth. As they grind the miles, the land seems deserted. There are few high mountain villages, and their inhabitants have either died or fled on one of the many hidden paths that led to Sassoun, which has always been the site of resistance and glory, the cradle of heroes for the fervid Armenian imagination.

One evening, when they feel particularly exhausted, they stop in a little village perched on the side of a mountain. They usually keep their distance, approaching only in the evening when they see neither lights nor smoke, and hear no voices. That particular evening, however, they are all so tired and hungry that they decide to approach the area immediately, while there is still light. That way they can see if they can find some leftover food, stored vegetables, or dried fruit hanging in a pantry corner.

When they get to the first houses, Makarios, who is at the head of the line, suddenly stops and puts a finger to his lips. "There is someone here," he says in a low voice. "Smoke is rising from the chimney of that home back there." They all draw near and see that Makarios is right. A wisp of smoke is rising into that serene twilit air that bears the forgotten smell of roasted meat. "It's lamb," whispers Hovsep enthusiastically. "Oh boy, lamb!" He drops Anoush's hand for once and begins to run heedless of everything but his hunger.

The others follow him, throwing caution to the wind, overcome by the soft spiral of that forgotten smell that surrounds them and drives them crazy. On the sides of the narrow and rocky street, like a silent admonition, stand two ancient, majestic *khatchars* that are so moss-grown that one can hardly see the flowers and fruits that surround the cross. The silent angel sits calmly at the foot of one of them. Only Anoush sees him, but she does not speak. She is, however, reassured and hurries along toward the lit fire.

The door is open. In the back, there is a man bent over the fireplace. He is an old man with long gray hair and heavy shepherd boots. He is completely engrossed in the roasting of his lamb. With a long feather, he seems to caress the already golden back that glitters in the darkness. Then he carefully places it on the stone and turns around. He sees the little group that has arrived and his face lights up, but he does not speak.

"Who are you, shepherd?" Kohar asks politely. "Whoever you are, let us stay here for the night and share your food. We are poor people, we are tired and hungry, as you can see, and there is also a child." The man is quiet and looks at her. A bushy beard covers his chin. Makarios adds his voice to Kohar's plea. "Help us, please. Do you live here? What village is this? And where are all the others?"

Hovsep, meanwhile, has sat down, on the edge of the stone that protrudes from the fireplace. The man, it seems, pays no attention to him. Eleni, and finally Anoush too, approach. Eleni looks at him fixedly, wondering at his silence. "What's wrong, old man? Have they harmed you?"

The man tries at first to elude her penetrating gaze, then lets himself fall on the stone, makes a strange sound, and opens his mouth. In that blackened cavity they see the stub of a tongue.

Chapter Twenty

They all look at him with fear, but the man closes his mouth and smiles. He then begins to gesticulate. No one understands what he is trying to say. "Does he want to tell us that there are soldiers around?" Makarios hypothesizes impatiently. Eleni shuts him up, and begins to ask questions to which the old man could respond with a yes or no. "Are you Armenian?" It is, naturally, the first crucial question. At his nod, she fires other questions until it becomes clear that the man had been tortured and his tongue cut off. He had survived only because they had thought him dead. No one was left in the village. All of its inhabitants had been killed by steel or fire.

As soon as he realizes that he is not alone in a deserted world, that other Armenians had also managed to survive, the man begins to tell his story with gestures. He is eager to share, to tell. It is like a river in full spate, and at one point, forgetting all about his roast, he takes Kohar's hand, and drags her toward a clearing at the edge of the village that had been blackened by fire. The others follow. There had been a large barn here, he explains, mimicking things and facts, where the women had taken refuge. They were burned alive there, as the soldiers laughed at their screams.

No one speaks as his hands draw the flames, the bodies, and the desperate screams in the air. As he ends his story he writes his name in the sand: Zacharias. It is then that Hovsep, who had stayed seated in front of the fireplace contemplating the lamb, breaks the spell and calls out nervously. He is hungry and can't wait any more.

At that, they all snap out of the tale and go to eat. Zacharias expertly takes the lamb off the fire and cuts the steaming meat. They sit on the ground around the fireplace, chewing, and for a moment their fears are appeased and they dare to believe in a possible future.

Consoled and warm, they hold a war council of sorts. How to reach territories under Russian control? How to get past the high mountains? Reaching the small village where they were sitting had already been tempting fate, but the very high mountains before them close in on each other, and the passes are steep and invisible to those who do not know the way. None of the five has ever been that far east.

Old Zacharias is quiet and listens. Then he stands and with a majestic gesture places an open palm on his chest. "I," and they all understand him as though he were speaking, "I know the way." With another gesture, he then points to the far-off mountain tops with his right hand extended, telling them, "I will take you to safety." Finally, with ancient pride, he crosses both hands on his chest to make his vow and then raises them toward the heavens, calling them to bear witness to it.

"We entrust ourselves to you and will come with you," Makarios says on everyone's behalf. But Kohar stands up, casts a quick glance around the room, and adds, "We bear a precious trust. We saved the Book of Moush." She solemnly unwraps the fabric and shows him the frontispiece. An enigmatic, rectangular drawing appears. It takes up the whole page, which is filled with colors and a thousand intertwined characters. It looks like the entryway to the enchanted castle of Scripture: an entire enclosure of crenellations resting on four thin, graceful, little columns—each different from the other—formed by flowers, fruits, and motley little beasts. Every detail, when inspected up close, is a joyful surprise; the elegant columns hover over the page, while the spaces they enclose are filled with lines and lines of Armenian letters, as though the writing itself were an essential part of the a harmonious and complex figurative world, intelligible even to simple souls.

The upper part is like a sumptuous carpet. Its drawings of real and imaginary animals—lions, deer, unicorns—facing each other and lacings and elegant racemes of beautiful flowers shimmer in their vivid colors. In the middle there is a mysterious light-blue circle that flutters with delicate arabesques that intertwine and form a thousand volutes. At the top, balancing on top of the crenellations, to the right and left, two pairs of animals with long, curved horns fiercely face each other. They seem to be perched on or, better yet, almost flying above the long line of wise words written in 1202 by the old scribe Vartan, of the Avakvank Monastery near Erzynka. His name is written in the book, like that of Stepanos, the miniaturist.

Like a shield on the right-hand side of the entire page, a very high cross, thin as a reed, stands guard. There are three tiny decorated cusps on top of the cross, formed by an infinite number of tightly interwoven knots, and intricate floral spirals.

They all look at it and get lost in the dream of a brimming, enclosed, and sheltered garden, filled with sweetness and surprises, of running water and fragrant roses. "Do you see the angels?" a fascinated Hovsep asks while his finger traces two disparate faces set in the thick weave of colors, palmettes, and spirals on the left, which seem to represent divine wisdom.

"And you, do you see the lions?" Kohar responds from the other side. "They are Armenian lions, the smiling kind, with scarves around their necks."

Even Zacharias gets lost in contemplation, and then smiles again. With more strength, as though a heavy load had just been lifted off of him, he kneels. He bends all the way down to the floor. He first presses his lips, then his forehead, to the book, his eyes closed.

Then they all kneel, one after the other, the three women and the boy. Makarios, the strong man, the cunning Greek, kneels last, almost reluctantly. He cannot help it. It is as though, at that very moment, a mysterious wind has come to blow through the valley, carrying the fragrances, the smells, the colors of the lost people, who are becoming ash and leaven for the land down below, in the entire valley of Moush. "We shall not perish, so long as the book exists," says the wind, as light as a whisper, like the voice of God.

Chapter Twenty-One

The next day, they set out with renewed courage. They are convinced that old Zacharias is the angel—a bit wounded, perhaps—who has answered their prayers, and they want to be worthy of him.

Zacharias takes the boy by the hand and walks with him. They don't need words; the mute man just clutches Hovsep's little hand when he wants to point something out, and they understand each other very well. With his other hand, he holds onto Anoush, who struggles to carry on. She has circles under her eyes, and her hands are sweaty. Every so often, she shrugs her shoulders as if something were bothering her.

Zacharias watches her and understands. He stops and assertively takes the weight that is burdening her and puts it on his shoulders. From that point on, he will be the one who carries it. Then he unscrews his flask, makes her take a sip of water, and gently pushes her forward, pointing to Hovsep and the path. With the back of his rough hand he caresses her cheek, tucks a lock of her hair behind her ear, and gazes at her intensely. He then puts a finger to his lips and looks at the others, communicating the need to be silent.

No one speaks. They follow their silent guide almost hypnotically through valleys and abandoned villages, through the ancient paths of Kurdish shepherds, day after day, silently putting one foot in front of the other, and their thoughts unravel as their minds focus on the few vital issues: drinking, eating, and sleeping.

Zacharias, though, never seems to sleep. During the day he guides them, and at night he is their guard. His austere face strikes fear—and melancholy—in everyone, and no one speaks to him, not even when they lie down under the stars at night. Anxious nocturnal sighs wordlessly communicate everyone's nightmares.

At sunset on the seventh day of walking, they spy some scattered houses in the distance and some people. They have arrived at the once-prosperous city of Erzerum on the Russian border. Erzerum used to be inhabited by many Armenians. It is now a battleground: the Russians and the Turks contend for it. When the Russians advance, the survivors of the Armenian massacres return with them, meditating revenge; when the Turks counterattack, the Armenians closely follow the retreating Russians. Armed gangs devastate whatever is left. There are famine and despair for all.

The desolate houses whose doors have been smashed, whose paneless windows stare like blind eyes in the night and stand exposed to outsiders, have been invaded by

the miserable complement of every army: money chang-
ers, prostitutes, gangs. People of all stripes, whose only
common ground is greed and anguish. Ottoman and
German officers in dress uniforms proudly make their
way through the filthy crowd. Every one of them has in
his house—in the beautiful homes confiscated from the
deportees—at least one Armenian to give him pleasure
and to satisfy his needs. The poor women, who have
lost everything but can at least eat their fill, furtively
exchange information and do what they can to help the
abandoned children who wander about in herds, rum-
maging through trash, and lacking the courage to ask
for bread. Summer will end soon and food will become
even scarcer.

And yet, even there in that hell, a small survival market, an extreme form of mutual support, flourishes. In
the shadows of dark nights, demons and angels wander
about, doors are opened and things quietly exchanged.
Zacharias, who knows many people in the city, knows
exactly where to go. He has everyone rest behind an
abandoned barn hidden by a thicket of hazelnut bushes.
When evening comes, he signals that they must be
careful and quiet, and he leads them to one of the last
houses and has them sit in a thriving orchard, under
a low window in the kitchen, which is illuminated by
the fire.

A woman is there, at work, and passes in front
of the window a few times. She is preparing something.
The scent of caramel, a scent from far-off times, fills

the air. Kohar gets a lump in her throat and suddenly feels faint. A modulated and sweet whistle breaks the silence, and the woman turns left and right while her eyes fill with tears. She furiously wipes them and shakes her head. But the whistle is repeated, and the woman is filled with hope and whispers, "Can that be you, Zacharias? Are you alive?"

With a commanding gesture, Zacharias has them all stay low, and he climbs through the window and enters the kitchen. A long silence follows, then a muffled cry. After a bit of time, the woman leans out in the dark and quietly hands them a loaf of bread and a jug of water. "I have nothing else for tonight," she says. "Tomorrow my lieutenant will leave for two days, and I'll let you in. In the meanwhile, sleep behind the house and make no noise. He'll leave through the front door. If he sees you, remember, I know nothing of you. Make sure you don't tell him that we've spoken. He's very jealous."

Chapter Twenty-Two

This is a story with a happy ending, despite it all. The Book of Moush will be saved. But much hardship and many adventures still await the humble heroes of this story. Their destinies will separate them once they are in Erzrum.

The storyteller is, however, becoming tired of telling the infinite tragedy of the Lost Homeland. Lamenting it does not bring peace to the Armenian survivors, who have been tossed here and there throughout the vast world, who will always miss their sweet orchards and lavish grain, their dances and gentle spouses, their high valleys and the slow rivers that cross them. The storyteller has exhausted her tears and wants to tell other stories.

But in midst of disaster and loss shine the saved books. By mysterious and secret paths, through labor and pain, like a river of gold, the manuscripts with their beautiful bindings, the shimmering illuminations with their small colorful worlds, palmette borders, crosses, and pomegranates, navigated this final ocean of pain and survived. They were brought to safety by the rough and wounded hands of all those suffering mothers who, step after step, reached the remote monasteries of the Caucasus, the crystal churches that so enchanted travelers, and finally Etchmiadzin, the center of all Armenian spirituality, the Holy Seat where the Only Begotten One descended and where the *katholikos*, the supreme patriarch, lives.

If we know the medieval splendors of this ancient civilization today, we owe it to the silent passion of these courageous and indomitable women who lost everything but their love for their great past. Thus it is also for the largest of all Armenian manuscripts, the Book of Moush, whose story I am telling.

The next morning, the strong Kohar is burning with a sudden fever. Eleni and Anoush try in vain to help her. They moisten her lips with a handkerchief soaked in water and vinegar. Her fever rises quickly, and Kohar quickly becomes delirious. "Bury me with the book," she repeats. "Dig a deep hole. I won't be cramped in there. No one will come to look for me there, only the angels of God, who will descend from Heaven on the day of the Resurrection of the Dead. I will press the book to my chest, and I will no longer struggle to carry it. Christ will see it, and I will be saved."

Everyone silently approaches her, trying to quiet her down. They whisper peace in her ear. Kohar continues to fret and is covered in sweat. The hours pass, and she seems a bit calmer. But her cheeks are covered with red blotches, and her eyes are immense. Her fever, Eleni believes, is even higher. Anoush whimpers, curled up at Kohar's feet with Hovsep, who is frightened and also has a face that has become red, for he keeps hiding it under Anoush's skirt.

Makarios is sitting a ways off, chewing on a rind of hard cheese. In the depths of his heart, he still hopes that their incredible voyage is coming to an end and that he and Eleni can still survive together. Oh, how he wishes to return with her to the Chora of Paros and grow old with her, far from the misfortunes of the Armenians!

Eleni, though, has other things on her mind. If Kohar dies, who will carry the book in her place? Or will they do what she wants? Will they bury it with her? It is more important to save the book, Eleni believes, than her own useless life. She does not think about Makarios.

Finally the woman of the house appears. She doesn't smile but rather signals for them to enter. By now it is day, and the orchard conceals them. They are, however, standing so still that they look like a block of marble. They quietly open the little chicken door and timidly enter the house.

The woman, whose name is Esther, expresses her fear and anguish. "But there are five of you! Where will I put you up?" Turning to Zacharias, who is watching and smoking in the corner, she yells, "You're simply crazy. You need to get to work and split up the group. I can only keep them here for today."

She had not yet noticed Kohar. When she sees her, with her intensely red cheeks and her shivering from feverish chills, she makes the Sign of the Cross. Her eyes fill with tears. "She has typhus, can't you see?" she says. "Many have it in the city. My sister died three days ago. She was living with me, and with the officer." She smiles, embarrassed, but no one minds. Then, speaking more quietly, she adds, "She'll hang on for a few more hours. Leave her to me."

Just then, Kohar begins to speak feverishly again. First, she asks again to be buried with the book so that Christ will recognize her on the day of the Resurrection of the Dead. Then she takes Eleni's hand and with sudden lucidity tells her: "No, this isn't right. The book must not die, but leave it with me for now so that I can present myself with it to God's judgment. Bury it with me. When all of this has passed, and *only* then, come back and take it. You'll find it intact, because I will have protected it well. Then bring it to the Holy Seat of Etchmiadzin, and tell them that it is a living treasure, and that I saved it with my life."

In tears, Eleni promises to do so, and Kohar closes her eyes and gives in to the lethargy. She will not wake up again.

Chapter Twenty-Three

Kohar's death throws everyone into confusion. Eleni goes to the orchard to cry in peace. Anoush joins her. Wringing her hands nervously, but with live, blazing, and determined eyes, Anoush says, "Now it's my turn. I need to continue the journey; I must take my part of the book to Etchmiadzin. I will only be able to rest there."

"Sister," Eleni says, "I will not abandon you. We will fulfill our destiny together." In the meanwhile, she reflects on how to break the news to Makarios, who waits trustingly as he chews on his cheese rind. Esther, though, moves about quickly, and everything becomes frantic. There is no way to have Kohar's body blessed. There are no more priests around. So in the afternoon, they wrap her body in an old sheet and bury it under the big pomegranate tree in the most protected corner of the garden, with its high wall. The officer will not return before tomorrow, but it is best to make haste.

Makarios and Zacharias work quickly in absolute silence. The others stand by watching, overcome by fear of the future, and resting a bit. They drink the pure water from the spring and rinse off the dust of the road. They place the book, wrapped in a bright cloth and layers and layers of straw to protect it, in her arms. On her eyes, they place fresh myrtle leaves to accompany her on her journey; on her forehead, they place a small cross. Kohar needs nothing else.

Then they hold their last war council. "The Russians are coming," Esther says with certainty. "I heard my officer speaking to his friend. He is not an evil man, but his hands are dripping with blood. There's Armenian blood everywhere in this city. I'm waiting for the right moment and will then hide and wait for them. I already know where to go. What are you going to do?"

She looks at Zacharias, and Zacharias looks at her. Everyone understands. Now that they have found each other again, the two will try their luck together. He opens his hands entreatingly, conveying what his mutilated mouth can no longer pronounce: they will keep each other company; they will try to give each other some warmth, a bit of forgetfulness.

Anoush kneels down in front of him and solemnly thanks him. She then takes her half of the book and puts it back on her shoulders. She takes Hovsep's hand and says in a low voice, "I'm leaving, then. May God and His Holy Mother accompany me."

Eleni springs up and says, "We're going with you, right, Makarios? She'll never make it on her own."

Makarios spits his rind angrily on the ground. For a moment he seems to be on the verge of saying something. Then he swallows noisily, stands up, and sighs. "Let's go, then," he says. "We don't have much time to waste."

Evening falls. It is time. Esther prepares a little bag with some nuts and bread, pulls out a blanket and a pair of the officer's heavy socks, puts a cap on Hovsep's head that is far too big for him (the child protests indignantly), and makes the Sign of the Cross on his forehead. Then she opens the door and whispers, "Go," and closes the door with a big sigh of relief. Seated on the wall of the crumbling house in front of them, the silent angel finally smiles.

Epilogue

And now, patient reader, we have finally arrived at the end of the story of the Book of Moush. While our simple heroes are crossing the front line on a dark, starless night, a Turkish patrol surprises them in their sleep. The wing of the silent angel grazes Eleni and Makarios just in time. Together, they throw their blanket over the sleeping Anoush, jump into the thicket, and let themselves be killed without complaint.

Anoush takes the child and flees east in the dark. Walking uninterruptedly, she manages to cross the high mountains of the Caucasus while carrying the book and keeping little Hovsep close. Anoush will also have to use the pickax that she had carried with her since the night of the massacres in her village. She will deliver a single, deadly blow to a shepherd who wanted to rape her in front of the boy.

In the end, she reaches the plains of Mount Ararat. Her destination is close. She must reach Etchmiadzin; only there can she deposit her heavy burden. She hands it over to a monk whose assignment is to receive and record the precious illuminated manuscripts carried to safety by many of the surviving women. He does not write down Anoush's name. She is just one of many.

When the Russians conquer Erzerum, Esther takes aside a czarist officer, whom she had hosted in her home. He has a kind, open face that inspires confidence: she reveals the secret of the buried book. Together they dig up Kohar's grave underneath the pomegranate tree and with pious hands remove the parcel with the book. They brush away the rotten straw, and the colors shine, as if coming back to life.

The officer takes care of the book, and when the Russian army retreats, he takes it with him to Tbilisi. Some years later, both halves of the book are finally reunited. They now rest together in Yerevan, the capital of Armenia, in the great Matenadaran library. And with the book shines the memory of Anoush and Kohar, the strong women of Moush.

Historical Note

The story of the rescue of the Homilary of Moush, the largest surviving Armenian manuscript, has for many years traveled through Armenian memories and legends. It—like Franz Werfel's epic of Musa Dagh (the mountain of Moses)—is one of the few stories that are a source of pride and honor for this defeated and humiliated people. Now dispersed in every corner of the world, having been almost completely destroyed by the 1915 genocide, the Armenians have had their ancestral land taken from them forever.

Even the architectural monuments—the "crystal churches" (as Cesare Brandi described them), the gigantic stone crosses, the palaces, and the ancient cemeteries of a once-great civilization—were demolished year after year with harsh thoroughness and blind determination. This is why the miraculous physical survival of that famous manuscript of 1202, the treasure of the Holy Apostles Monastery, has taken on such great symbolic importance.

The high valley of Moush is not far from Lake Van. Isolated and flat, rich and fertile thanks to the many rivers that flow through it, it is encircled by impervious mountains. Toward the end of 1915, almost all of its Armenian inhabitants—about one hundred thousand people: men, women, and children—were slaughtered.

The massacres at Moush and other villages in the valley were bloodcurdling. Very few survivors, women and children especially, were able to reach Russian-occupied territory.

According to the most widely diffused legend, two women found the book in the rubble of the monastery and carried it to safety by dividing it into two. One of the women died, after having buried her half of the book. That half was discovered by a Russian officer and taken to Tbilisi, while the other half was taken to Yerevan and given to the monks of Etchmiadzin.

The book was put back together in the 1920s. A few of its pages, removed in the nineteenth century, are conserved in the collection of the Mekhitarist fathers in Venice and Vienna.

Until a few years ago, very few details of the massacre of Moush were known. In recent years, several crucial eyewitness accounts of the events have been published. These include the firsthand accounts of the Swedish nurse Alma Johansson and her Norwegian colleague Bodil Katharine Biørn. The two women ran an orphanage in Moush, and their charges were literally ripped from their hands and killed. Bodil Biørn also took a series of startling photographs, including a tender one from 1916 of a group of girls dressed in festive clothes, each with a doll in her hand, and some twenty shots of the terrible misery of the women who survived.

These events, these images, stirred memories and recollections of stories I heard in Aleppo many years ago that were buried in me.

This story was born from them. May the patient reader accept it like a fruit from Armenia—a winter pomegranate or a sweet apricot—and taste it as one tastes Armenian fairy tales on a winter night around the hearth. These fairy tales always begin with an auspicious phrase that prepares everyone for the tale:

Once upon a time, there was and there was not . . .

And they would end like this:

Three apples fall from the sky: the first for the storyteller; the second for the listener; the third for the whole world.

a.a.

Bibliography

Bibliography on the Armenian tragedy is huge. Hundreds of memoirs, testimonies, diaries, and accounts of both survivors and foreign eyewitnesses, as well as photographs, archival materials, and historical works, are now at the disposal of scholars. For the specific history of the Valley of Moush (one of the cradles of Armenian civilization) and the events of 1915, I have listed a few fundamental texts:

Akçam, Taner. *Killing Orders: Talat Pasha's Telegrams and the Armenian Genocide* (Palgrave Studies in the History of Genocide). Cham: Palgrave Macmillan, 2018.

de Bellaigue, Christopher. *Rebel Land: Unraveling the Riddle of History in a Turkish Town*. New York: Penguin, 2010.

Hovannisian, Richard G., ed. *Armenian Baghesh/ Bitlis and Taron/Moush*. UCLA Armenian History and

Cultural Series. Cosa Mesa, CA: Mazda Publishers, 2001.

Nash-Marshall, Siobhan. *The Sins of the Fathers: Turkish Denialism and the Armenian Genocide*. New York: Crossroads (Herder & Herder), 2018.

Orfalian, Sonya, ed. *Le mele dell'immortalità. Fiabe armene*. Milan: Guerini and Associates, 2000. (I quote Orfalian's work by heart in the final lines of this book.)

Ter Minassian, Anahide. "Un exemple, Mouch 1915." In *Actualité du Génocide des Arméniens*. Paris: Edipol, 1999.

* * * * *

Information on the two Northern European nurses and the photographs taken by Bodil Katharine Biørn, as well as the story of the Saint Arakelots Monastery and the Book of Moush, can easily be found online. Beautiful and ancient songs of the Valley of Moush can be found on YouTube, as can a few photos from before the genocide.